Harm held her gaze for a long moment, his hand tight on her arm. "What if whoever is playing these games gets more personal?"

Talia lifted her chin, her entire body tingling now. Why couldn't he let go of her and sever the electric current racing along her nerve endings? "What do you mean, more personal?" she asked, her voice breathy. She cleared her throat and continued. "I'd say attacking my clients is already pretty personal."

"What if someone corners you?" He backed her against the wall. "Are you prepared to fight for your life? Do you know how to defend yourself?"

Her body hummed with the electricity burning through her nerves and veins. "I think I can," she whispered, her gaze shifting to Harm's lips. Holy hell, she had the sudden urge to kiss them. What was wrong with her?

Harm shook his head. "There is a difference between thinking and knowing." He bent close. "I can show you some moves."

She ran her tongue over her suddenly dry lips. "I'm sure you can..."

FOUR RELENTLESS DAYS

New York Times **Bestselling Author**

ELLE JAMES

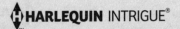

HARLEQUIN INTRIGUE®

To my editor, Denise Zaza—thank you for your continued faith in me as an Intrigue author and for all your support and reassurance.

To my daughter Courtney Paige for helping brainstorm plots. I love you so very much and wish you great success in your own writing.

To my readers who keep coming back for more. You're the reason I do what I do. Thank you for being so faithful and encouraging.

ISBN-13: 978-1-335-52660-1

Four Relentless Days

Copyright © 2018 by Mary Jernigan

Recycling programs for this product may not exist in your area.

Printed in U.S.A.

HARLEQUIN®
www.Harlequin.com

Elle James, a *New York Times* bestselling author, started writing when her sister challenged her to write a romance novel. She has managed a full-time job and raised three wonderful children, and she and her husband even tried ranching exotic birds (ostriches, emus and rheas). Ask her, and she'll tell you what it's like to go toe-to-toe with an angry 350-pound bird! Elle loves to hear from fans at ellejames@earthlink.net or ellejames.com.

Books by Elle James

Harlequin Intrigue

Mission: Six

One Intrepid SEAL
Two Dauntless Hearts
Three Courageous Words
Four Relentless Days

Ballistic Cowboys

Hot Combat
Hot Target
Hot Zone
Hot Velocity

SEAL of My Own

Navy SEAL Survival
Navy SEAL Captive
Navy SEAL to Die For
Navy SEAL Six Pack

Visit the Author Profile page at Harlequin.com.

CAST OF CHARACTERS

"Harm" Harmon Payne—US Navy SEAL. For a big guy, he's light on his feet and fast. Good at silent entry into buildings.

Talia Montclair—Owner/operator of the All Things Wild Resort in Kenya. Her husband was killed by a raging rhinoceros, leaving Talia to run the resort single-handed.

John Krause—Owner/operator of the resort neighboring All Things Wild Resort in Kenya.

Raila Gakuru—Local Kenyan witch doctor.

"Buck" Graham Buckner—US Navy SEAL, team medic. Went to medical school but didn't finish. Joined the navy and became a SEAL.

"Diesel" Dalton Samuel Landon—US Navy SEAL. Gunner and team lead.

"Pitbull" Percy Taylor—US Navy SEAL, tough guy who doesn't date much. Raised by a taciturn marine father. Lives by rules and structure. SOC-R boat captain.

"Big Jake" Jake Schuler—US Navy SEAL, demolitions expert. Good at fine fingerwork.

"T-Mac" Trace McGuire—US Navy SEAL, communications man, equipment expert.

Dr. Angela Vega—Provides medical care for people in South Sudan with Doctors Without Borders. Fell in love with a fellow medical student and was crushed when he left medical school and her without a word. Sworn off falling in love again.

Marly Simpson—Bush pilot in Africa. Her father was a bush pilot and taught her to fly. Her mother teaches children in the poor villages of Africa.

Mr. Wiggins—All Things Wild Resort's mascot, a leopard.

Chapter One

First night back at the All Things Wild Safari and Resort in Kenya, Africa, and Harmon "Harm" Payne had trouble sleeping. Their commander had granted the team a bonus week of vacation. After a particularly difficult mission in South Sudan, cleaning up the damage done by a ruthless warlord bent on wreaking havoc with the locals and stealing their children for his army, the SEAL team deserved this time to unwind.

Though his week of rest and relaxation had begun, he couldn't rest or relax and paced the sleek wooden floors of his cabin, hoping to get sleepy, but so far, nothing was working.

As a US Navy SEAL, he was used to snatching some shut-eye whenever he had fifteen minutes to spare. Why couldn't he do it now?

He stood by the window, staring out into the darkness of night, studying the myriad of stars twinkling in the heavens. The setting was perfect, the mission had been a success, but he couldn't calm his racing pulse. Harm felt on edge, as if he teetered on the precipice of something.

He lay on the bed, forced his eyes to close and counted bullets, hoping the monotony of the numbers would lull him to sleep. Around fifty, he must have slipped into a troubled sleep. The numbers became the beat of a drum; the sleek bullets became gyrating bodies, shiny with sweat and paint, dancing in the flames of a bonfire. The rhythm grew stronger, the dancing more erratic, and a voice called out words in a language he could not understand. A flowing red scarf drifted through the dancers and into the fire, becoming part of the dancing flames.

What did it mean? Why was he there?

A movement in the shadows surrounding the fire caught his attention. The face of a coyote, wolf or jackal appeared, its golden eyes reflecting the glow of the burning embers.

For a moment, Harm's attention remained riveted on the jackal, his heart beating fast and furious, slamming against his ribs, as if eager to escape the jackal and the confines of his ribs.

Harm swayed with the drumbeat, his body drawn like a moth to the flames, his gaze captivated by the jackal's eyes, mesmerized in the effect of the dancing flames. His feet moved as if of their own volition, taking him to within reach of the blaze. He would have fallen in had an owl not swooped low, screeching loudly at just that moment.

The sound jerked him back from the fire. The

jackal disappeared and Harm sat up in the bed, his heart racing at the close call in the dream. He rubbed his eyes, swung his feet over the side and stood, letting the night air cool his sweating body.

Obviously, sleep wasn't coming any time soon. At least, not the restful kind he sorely needed.

Closing his eyes now would only bring on a recurrence of the freaky nightmare. Harm pulled on a T-shirt, jeans and boots and left his cabin for the main house, hoping to find a sandwich or a beer. Maybe that would help settle his nerves and let him sleep…dream-free.

In the distance, he heard the scream of something that sounded like a big cat. The night sounds of the savanna were enough to make anyone a little nervous. He was glad he wasn't sleeping in a tent, exposed to whatever wild animal sniffed him out as a potential meal.

His buddy Buck had been on a recon mission with his doctor lady for a couple days, sleeping in the open, exposed to the elements and wild creatures of South Sudan. They'd managed to survive, with the worst threat being from the warlord they were determined to find and nail.

Surely Harm would be okay walking by himself between the cabin and the main lodge without being stalked by a hungry beast.

Talia had mentioned walking in pairs to discourage the wildlife from singling them out, but he didn't want to wake any of his teammates. They didn't have problems with insomnia, apparently.

Harm followed the starlit path to the lodge and climbed the stairs to the front door. As he reached for the door handle, a high-pitched scream pierced the night air, followed by a long wailing cry.

His hand jerked backward and he spun toward the sound.

"It's just a jackal," a feminine voice said from the shadows on the wide veranda. "They like to yodel at night."

Harm turned toward the sound.

Talia Ryan, the resort owner, rose from a porch swing and leaned against the railing, the starlight glinting off her blue-black hair. Beside her lay the resort mascot, Mr. Wiggins, the long, sleek leopard they'd met on their previous visit.

The animal lay stretched out across the decking, completely relaxed and asleep.

"You get used to the sound of the jackals after a while," Talia said.

"Apparently Mr. Wiggins is unconcerned."

Talia laughed. "He feels safe here."

The jackals screamed again, making Harm start.

Talia looked out into the night. "And if it's not the jackals, it's the lions chuffing or the elephants trumpeting. There really isn't such a thing as a quiet night on the savanna." She turned toward him. "Are the natives keeping you awake?"

He chuckled, though the sound was strained, even

to his own ears. Her comment hit far too close to home for comfort. He shrugged it off. "I wish I could blame it on the animal noises, but I just couldn't sleep. What's your excuse?"

She shrugged, the slight movement unaffected yet graceful. "Some nights I don't sleep well. There just happen to be more of them lately."

Harm admired the curvy silhouette of the beautiful woman, glad for something besides flames, dancing bodies and jackals swirling through his mind. "What would keep a pretty lady like you up at night?"

She stiffened, her gaze turned toward the night and the savanna where the jackal sang. "Nothing my guests need to worry about."

Harm should have left the conversation there and entered the main lodge in search of that snack, but something kept him on the veranda with Talia.

He liked the woman who owned and managed the resort single-handedly in a country where native women were often treated worse than cattle. "I imagine you have a lot of responsibilities, running a resort by yourself. Is this something you've always wanted to do?"

She laughed. "It wasn't *my* dream."

"No? Then whose dream was it?"

She hesitated for a long moment before finally answering, "It was my husband's."

"Husband?" Harm hadn't heard anything about a

husband in connection with Talia during the several days they'd spent at the resort a couple weeks before.

"Michael was a freelance photographer. We spent so much of our time here in Africa, we decided to buy the resort and make it permanent."

"Where is he now?" Harm asked.

"He was killed by a rhinoceros over a year ago." Her voice was soft, quiet, almost a whisper. But the tone said it all.

The catch in her voice tugged at Harm's heart. "You miss him still?"

She nodded. "For the first few months, I could barely breathe. I knew life on the savanna could be dangerous, but I never thought I'd lose Michael to the animals he fought so hard to save. He always seemed so good with them. And they were tolerant and accepting of him."

"They don't call them wild for nothing," Harm pointed out.

She nodded. "Still, it was so sudden. One day he was here, the next he was gone. We'd been together since we were teenagers. I really had no idea how to go on without him."

"You seem to be doing fine now."

She shook her head. "I didn't take reservations for over six months, and when I did, I only invited a few guests at a time. My heart wasn't into it. Not without Michael."

"You always seem so upbeat around us."

"I never stopped missing him, but it's easier to get

through the days now than it was after it first happened. The guests keep me from getting sad." She turned to him. "So thank you."

The starlight shined down on her face, illuminating her bright eyes, making them sparkle despite the melancholy droop to her lips.

Harm had the sudden urge to pull the woman into his arms, to hold her and make the hurt go away. But she was still grieving for her husband. It wouldn't be right for him to embrace her.

She dipped her chin. "I guess I miss him more at night, when I slow down from the day's activities. The past week has been particularly difficult with everything happening at once."

Harm couldn't resist. He opened his arms. "I'm not your husband, but I have strong arms."

She gave him a wobbly smile and stepped into his embrace. "Thanks." Talia rested her hands on his chest and pressed her forehead to his breastbone. "I didn't realize how much I missed having a hug."

"My pleasure," he said, his tone soft, gentle, as calming as he could make it. The moment she'd stepped into his arms, he realized his mistake. He'd gone a while without female companionship. Her body pressed to his made him hyperaware of that neglect.

She was the perfect height, the top of her head coming up to just beneath his chin. He rested his hands at the small of her back, amazed at how narrow her waist was in comparison to the swell of her luscious hips and breasts. His blood heated and his groin tightened automatically.

Yeah, holding this woman, who still grieved her husband, might not be his smartest move.

For a long moment, Talia stood in his arms. Eventually, she turned her head and laid her cheek against his heart.

He pressed her closer, fully cognizant of even her slightest move. Conscious of his own proximity and desires, he fought to hold himself back from making an idiot of himself.

"Why are you still here at the resort? Why didn't you leave when your husband passed?" he asked.

She shrugged. "I loved Michael. Leaving here would have been like leaving him all over again. I thought about selling, but I just couldn't. This was his dream. He saw beauty in every living creature. For the most part, so did I. But when one of his beautiful creatures killed him, I had a hard time seeing them as purely beautiful."

Finally, he set her at arm's length and brushed a strand of her dark hair off her cheek, tucking it behind her ear. "Are you okay for now?"

She nodded and then looked up into his eyes. "You're kind. Thank you."

"For what? I should be thanking you. It's been a long time since I've held a beautiful woman in my arms." He clasped his hands together to keep from pulling her back against him.

"Look at us. All this talk about me and my lost love…what about you?" Talia asked.

Harm stiffened. "What about me?"

"You say you haven't held a woman in your arms for a long time." Talia pinned him with her wide-eyed stare. "Why not?"

His jaw tightened. "I have a job to do. Women aren't part of it."

"But you have to have someone to come home to."

"Why?" He waved his hand. "Don't answer that. My job precludes relationships. Besides, unlike you, I don't believe in true love. It doesn't exist."

"Oh, but it does." She touched his shoulder. "It's that feeling that you can't live without that person, that your life is better for having him in it."

"And when he leaves, sends you a Dear John letter, just walks out of your life or dies?"

She smiled. "You thank God you had him for the time you did."

"But you said you couldn't live without him. Yet, here you are." He raked her with his gaze. "You appear to be very much alive to me."

She chuckled. "I am. And I had to learn how to live without him, but I wouldn't trade my time with Michael for anything."

"If you believe in love, are you going to fall in love again? Knowing what could happen?"

"I don't know if love can happen for me again, but if it does, I'm not going to pass it up because I'm afraid of losing him. I'd be stupid to walk away when there is so much happiness to be gained."

"And so much sorrow…" he reminded her.

Talia nodded. "True, but feeling so deeply is a sign that we're very much alive. If I push past the sorrow, I remember the happiness and it's all worth it." She laughed. "I'm sorry. You're a guest. I shouldn't be bringing you down with my troubles."

"You didn't. I'm just curious. If you're finally getting over the sorrow, what's keeping you up at night? When we were here a couple weeks ago, other than the poachers, I didn't get the feeling you were unhappy."

"I wasn't." She stared out at the night again. "Everything seemed to be getting back on track. And then…strange things started happening."

He studied her silhouette, noting the frown pulling her brow lower. Normally Harm avoided deep conversations, preferring to remain uninvolved. But Talia had been through so much, and she seemed like a genuinely nice lady. He wanted to get to the bottom of her troubles. "Strange? Like strangers showing up? Or hinky strange?"

She laughed. "Hinky?" Her smile soon faded. "Actually, hinky kind of describes it."

"Really?"

"Yes." She stepped away from him and wrapped her arms around her middle. "As the locals would say, the resort has some bad juju going on."

Harm crossed to the swing and sat. He patted the

space beside him. "Tell me about this bad juju." If it was anything like what he'd been dreaming a few minutes ago, he could understand her concern.

She hesitated before joining him. As she settled, her movement set the swing in motion, gently swaying in the dark.

Again, Harm might have been better off going into the kitchen alone.

Talia's warm thigh rested against his, and with every sway of the swing, he caught a whiff of her perfume.

"Yesterday, we found native paintings on the doors of the cabins."

"Graffiti?" Harm asked.

"In a way. Only the content was threatening."

"How so?"

"They'd painted an owl swooping down over several people." She snorted. "Stick figures, nothing too dramatic, but enough to scare away the guests who'd been staying in the cabins."

"Why?"

"I had hired new guards to protect the perimeter. They swear they saw no one sneak past them into the compound. They got to the guests before I did and spooked them by telling them about what omen the images foretold."

"And what does an owl mean in the local folklore?"

She stopped the swing with a foot on the board of the veranda and stood. "It doesn't matter."

Harm stood and rested an arm over her shoulder, cupping her arm with his hand. "You can't scare me. I'm a crusty old SEAL. I don't believe in bad juju. But I do believe in bad people who like to frighten women and children."

She squared her shoulders, shrugging off his grip. "I'm not easily frightened, either, but when it scares my guests, it threatens me and my livelihood." She lifted her chin and faced Harm. "Around here, if an owl flies close to you or a loved one, it means someone is going to die."

"You don't believe that hooey, do you?"

"Normally I don't." She looked back over her shoulder toward him. "I believe people painted the signs over the doors. But it's hard to discount the omens when they happen."

"What do you mean?"

"The night before my husband died, an owl swooped over my head." She sighed. "I shrugged it off as coincidence…until they brought Michael back to the lodge the next day. Then I went through everything I could have done to keep him from dying that day."

"But you couldn't undo what was done," Harm said softly.

"No."

"And you think it's happening again?"

"I haven't seen an owl this time around, but someone is planting those superstitions in the heads of my staff and my guests. I can't run this place by myself.

If the juju threats continue, I won't have staff to take care of the guests and the guests will leave, like the ones who left the day your team arrived. I'll be out of business." Talia's voice lowered to a whisper. "My husband's dream will be lost."

Once again, Harm fought the urge to pull Talia into his arms. She had been so very upbeat and friendly from the day she'd first welcomed the SEALs to her resort.

Harm was a fixer. He liked to make things right. But he wasn't sure he could fix Talia's problems. He didn't have any experience with black magic and bad juju.

Chapter Two

Talia hadn't wanted to bring her new guest into the superstitious world of the locals. Granted, the SEALs seemed of stronger constitutions than her rich guests who'd left the day before, hurrying away because of a painting on their doors.

She stared up at the tall, broad-shouldered SEAL and wanted to laugh.

Harm would not be as easily frightened. Hell, he'd frighten those trespassers who'd dared to draw the omens on the doors. Perhaps having the SEALS there would keep the saboteurs from spreading their portents of bad juju on her property.

"Enough about my troubles." She pasted a smile on her lips. "Is there anything I can get you?"

"No. Like you told us from the beginning, we can make do for ourselves. I was heading for the kitchen, hoping to snag a sandwich."

"Do you mind if I join you?" she asked, not ready to be alone after everything that had happened. She'd found temporary comfort in this man's arms, something she hadn't counted on, especially after the loss of her husband. A tug of guilt pulled at her heart. At the same time, she felt a spark of something else. She refused to put a name to it. Not yet.

"I'd be honored." Harm offered her his elbow.

She slipped her hand into the crook of his arm and stepped through the door with him.

They had just crossed the threshold when a shot rang out. One of the cabin doors slammed open and Big Jake burst out running backward, wearing only his boxer shorts, cursing. He held his M4A1 rifle in his hand, pointed back into the cabin.

Pitbull, Diesel, Buck and T-Mac all ran out of their cabins in varying stages of undress, carrying their weapons.

"I heard a shot fired." T-Mac hurried toward Big Jake, wearing just his jeans, no shirt or shoes.

"Me too." Diesel joined him on the path, in shorts and nothing else.

"What's going on?" Pitbull asked, tugging a T-shirt over his head, his jeans pulled up but not buttoned.

Marly emerged seconds later, zipping up her flight suit. "Who's shooting?"

Harm leaped off the veranda and ran toward Big Jake. "What happened?"

Big Jake shook his head. "I've never seen one that big. It was curled up at the foot of my bed."

"What was curled up at the foot of your bed?" Harm asked as he arrived at Big Jake's side.

His teammate shook his head and pointed his rifle toward the door. "I was having this strange dream. Drums, painted dancers, incense… I was falling into a fire when I woke up, sat up and stared at a cobra coiled at the foot of my bed, his head up, hood spread and ready to launch himself at me. I did the only thing a good SEAL could do."

"You blew it away, right?" T-Mac shuddered.

"Damn right I blew it away." He shot a glance toward Talia. "I'm sorry if I also put a hole in the wall."

"Holy hell, I hate snakes," T-Mac said. "That would be one of my worst nightmares—forget the fire and dancers. Snakes are the devil."

Talia pushed past him, headed into the cabin, then paused at the door. "You did hit it, didn't you?"

"I'm pretty sure I did." Big Jake shoved a hand through his hair. "It was all pretty much a blur."

Harm caught her arm. "Let me go in first."

"Here." T-Mac handed him the pistol he'd brought from his cabin. "You'll need this."

Harm grinned. "Are you sure *you* don't want to make sure the snake is dead?"

T-Mac crossed his arms over his chest and shook his head. "No. I trust you to make it right."

"I can take care of this," Talia said. "We have the occasional snake enter the compound. Although not lately. The villagers see cobras on occasion. They like rats and chickens."

"And the occasional baby?" Marly asked, a shiver shaking her body.

Talia grimaced. "They don't usually eat the babies. But some children have been bitten on occasion."

"Nice," T-Mac said. "Nightmare, I'm telling you." He turned to Diesel. "Why did we decide a safari in Kenya was a good idea?"

"You wanted to come as much as the rest of us," Diesel reminded him. "At least you weren't stuck in the jungle along the Congo for several nights, sleeping in snake-infested trees."

"Enough talk about snakes." T-Mac raised a hand. "Who's for heading back to Djibouti and the friendly scorpions they have?"

"We're not going back to Djibouti," Harm said. "One snake is not a den of snakes."

"How do you know?" T-Mac asked.

"Shut up, T-Mac." Harm unlocked the safety on the handgun and stepped past Talia and through the door, switching on the light. "I'll let you know if there are more when I come out."

"*If* you come out alive," T-Mac muttered behind him.

Cobra bites were deadly if left untreated. But there was treatment, Harm coached himself. Although he wasn't horribly afraid of snakes like T-Mac, he had a healthy respect for them and the damage they could create with a single bite.

He edged his way into the sitting room, past an overturned end table and a twisted rug. Big Jake had been in a hurry to get out of the cabin. He couldn't blame the man. He probably would have reacted the same way if he'd awakened to a snake in his bed, much less a deadly cobra.

He searched every nook and cranny in the sitting room before entering the bedroom. As soon as he did, he noticed the long, sleek body of a serpent draped across the bed, its tail hanging over the side. A dark spatter of blood spread across the white comforter and the mosquito netting draped from the ceiling. He rounded the foot of the bed to the other side to check the other end of the snake before he could let go of the breath he'd been holding.

"Dead?" Talia asked from the door.

Harm jumped. "You were supposed to wait outside."

"You were taking a long time," she responded. "I got worried."

"I was making certain there wasn't another snake in the building. They can hide in the strangest places."

"You would know this because?" She arched her brows and crossed her arms over her chest.

"I grew up in a small town in Texas. We had our share of rat snakes, rattlers and copperheads. We'd find them in garages, barns and sheds. Sometimes they would make their way into the houses through an open door or window and curl up in the base of a flowerpot or shoebox."

"Nice." Talia studied the snake lying across the bed. "Looks like a spitting cobra. Big Jake's lucky the snake didn't spit in his eye—its spit can blind a person."

"Don't tell T-Mac. He'll have one more reason to be afraid of snakes, as if being bitten isn't enough."

Talia chuckled. "It's hard to imagine any of you SEALS afraid of anything."

"As a kid, T-Mac was traumatized by a snake. I think his mother made him hold one once. He's been terrified ever since."

"But you must have been in places with snakes before."

Harm continued his search of the room, dropping to his knees to check under the bed. He was careful, now that he was aware that cobras could spit. "Being a SEAL challenges every one of your fears, but thankfully, they don't stick you in a pit filled with snakes. I don't think the cadre liked snakes any more than anyone else, or they would have used them, too."

The space beneath the bed was free of snakes and surprisingly clean of dust.

"Do you keep all the cabins this clean?" Harm asked.

Talia laughed. "I'm worried about snakes and you're looking at how clean this place is?"

"I've been in hotels that don't clean as well as this. I don't see a single dust bunny, even in the corners."

"My staff keeps the entire compound clean. We pride ourselves in making it a beautiful place to stay for all visitors, not including deadly cobras." Talia opened the closet and checked inside.

Harm slipped up beside her, ready to shoot anything that moved. "Well, they'll have their work cut out for them, cleaning up snake parts."

"I'll probably handle it myself. I've had a hard enough time convincing them to stay after the paintings on the cabin doors. I had to scrub them off myself."

Harm could picture her cleaning the paint off the doors. "We'll help you get this place cleaned up."

"No way." She shook her head. "You are guests of mine. I won't have you doing the dirty work."

"We're kind of used to dirty work. It's what we do." He nodded toward the pillows. "If you don't mind sacrificing a pillowcase to the cause, I'll start by removing the offender from the premises."

"By all means." She shook a pillow out of its case and held it out for Harm.

He lifted the snake off the bed, dropped it into the case and then took it from her.

"Be careful you don't let the fangs touch you," she said. "They still contain poison."

Holding the bag away from his body, Harm checked all the closets, drawers and corners and then straightened. "I can take care of the cobra, just tell me where you want me to put him."

Talia shook her head and held out her hand. "I'll take him and put him in the freezer."

He kept his hold on the bag. "Please tell me you aren't cooking up cobra for dinner."

She laughed. "No, but I know they need antivenin. They might be able to milk a dead snake for its venom, which they use to make antivenin."

"You're a woman after my own heart." Harm followed her out of the cabin, careful not to touch her with the snake in the pillowcase. "Beautiful and practical." If he was in the market for a wife, she'd be an amazing catch. But then, he wasn't in the market for a relationship. Especially with a woman who had so completely believed in love.

Harm believed in lust, the natural, chemical reaction between a man and a woman. But love?

No. Absolutely not.

Oh, sure. Once upon a time he thought he had, but one Dear John letter cured him of that fallacy very quickly.

But that didn't keep him from wanting women. A man had urges, after all.

"IF YOU'LL FOLLOW ME…" Talia turned toward the lodge and then back to Big Jake. "And I have a room in the lodge for you, Big Jake."

He nodded. "Good thing, because I wasn't gonna sleep in there. No, ma'am."

She laughed. "I can't blame you. But no worries. We have a snake-free room upstairs with a comfortable bed."

"The cabin is clear, if you want to grab your gear," Harm said.

"Yeah." Big Jake frowned. "If you're sure."

"I'm sure. I even looked in your gear bag. No

more snakes." He held up the bag. "And you killed the one on your bed. He's not going to bother you again."

"Damn straight." Big Jake sucked in a breath and eyed the cabin, as if the structure might assume a life of its own.

"Come on," Diesel said. "I'll go with you."

"I can do it myself," Big Jake grumbled. "I just need a minute."

Talia fought back a grin. Seeing a huge SEAL like Big Jake hesitant to enter a building was so unlike the man. She could imagine him charging in like a bull at a bullfight.

Diesel draped an arm over the shaken man's shoulder. "Take all the time you need, dude. It's not every day you wake up to a cobra in your bed."

Big Jake grimaced. "And I hope it never happens again."

"We've got your back," T-Mac reassured him.

"Good," Big Jake said. "Then why don't you go in and get my gear?"

T-Mac backed away, shaking his head. "I said I've got your back, not your *bag*."

"If it makes you feel better," Talia said, "I've been in the rooms and didn't see any more snakes."

"I'm going. I'm going." Big Jake sucked in a deep breath and followed Diesel into the cabin.

"Let's get that snake on ice," Talia said.

Harm followed her into the lodge and through to the kitchen. She flipped on light switches along the way. Once in the massive, updated kitchen, Talia opened the door to the walk-in freezer and held it wide for Harm to carry the bag with the snake inside.

A cool blast of air chilled her hands and cheeks as she waited for Harm to step inside.

"Where do you want me to put him?" Harm asked.

"Let me get a box." Talia hurried to the pantry, found an empty box and returned to the walk-in freezer. "The far side has empty shelves. I'd like to keep him separated from the food we serve the guests."

Harm chuckled. "We'd like that, too. I wouldn't want your chef to confuse chicken and cobra."

"I'll warn them not to touch the bag in the box. I don't want the staff hurt by brushing up against the snake's fangs." Her lips twisted into a frown. "Maybe I shouldn't put the snake in this freezer."

"If there is a shortage of antivenin, saving this snake could help. You're doing the right thing," Harm assured her as he set the bag in the box and the box on a shelf in the farthest corner of the freezer.

When they emerged from the freezer, the kitchen was filled with the rest of Harm's team, plus Dr. Angela Vega and Marly.

Buck clapped his hands together. "Since we're all awake, we thought we'd come raid the refrigerator."

Talia smiled. "I can whip up a casserole in about forty minutes, or I had the chef prepare a ham earlier to make sandwiches for the safari tomorrow. I believe there's enough meat for snacks tonight and sandwiches tomorrow. It's up to you."

"Ham sandwiches sound great," Diesel said. "But we can help ourselves. You don't have to stay up on our account."

Talia smiled. "I wasn't asleep, and a sandwich sounds good to me, too." She pulled the container filled with ham slices out of the commercial refrigerator and set it on the counter. Then she laid out freshly baked bread, garden-grown lettuce and tomatoes, plates, utensils and condiments.

"We can take it from here," Buck said. "Thank you."

"While you are preparing sandwiches, I'll check the room upstairs for you, Big Jake." She turned to leave the kitchen, crossed the wide-open living area and mounted the stairs to the second floor.

Footsteps behind her made her turn back.

Harm climbed the steps a few feet behind her.

Talia stopped midway up the staircase. "Are you following me?"

He nodded. "With all the crazy things happening, I thought I'd check the room for uninvited guests."

"I can do that myself," she insisted. "I've lived here long enough to know what to look for."

"Would you have looked for a cobra in your bed?" he asked.

Talia shivered and pressed her lips into a tight line. "Probably not. We've never had that happen here at All Things Wild."

"Then humor me. Let me look first."

"You're not going to be around forever. I need to do these things on my own."

"I get that, but it would make me feel better to help, since I'm here already." He winked and waved her ahead. "Ladies first. At least to the bedroom door."

She led the way to the guest room she had in mind for Big Jake. "Maybe I should have all of you move into the lodge if things are getting...how did you say?"

"Hinky. If you have another room in the lodge, I'd like to snag it as well."

Talia paused in reaching for the door handle of a room. "Are you afraid of snakes, like T-Mac?"

Harm shook his head. "No, but I don't like that these things are happening to the resort. Someone is playing games with you. They might make it more personal."

In the back of her mind, Talia had thought the same thing, but she hadn't let the possibility take root until Harm voiced it. "You think someone is targeting my resort and me?"

Harm took her hand in his. "I don't know, but while we're here, let us help. Let *me* help."

"But you're my guests."

"In case you hadn't noticed, we're not your normal uppity clientele. We've slept in deserts, jungles and swamps. We've been shot at, had explosives go off nearby and nearly been killed so many times, you start to think you're invincible, or just that your number is not quite up yet."

"Yet," she whispered. "You never know when that might happen."

"Exactly. We could step on an improvised explosive device or be hit by a bus. We don't borrow trouble. We wait for it to come to us. But that doesn't mean we don't take precautions."

"Like?"

"We brought our own weapons. We're prepared to take on anything and anyone."

Talia smiled. "I'm kind of glad my guests left room for you and your team to stay." She nodded. "Thank you for offering to help. While you're here, I accept." She held out her hand. He engulfed it in his own, sending sparks of electricity throughout her body.

As quickly as she took his hand, she pulled hers free, heat suffusing her cheeks. "I'll just be a minute checking on this room and the one down the hall. Do you think T-Mac would like to stay in the lodge as well? Seeing as he's so afraid of snakes? I don't want him to be uncomfortable in one of the cabins. I can't imagine how that cobra got into Big Jake's room. These things never happened while Michael was alive."

Harm touched a finger to her lips. "I'll ask. In the meantime, let me check the rooms first."

Talia's lips tingled where his finger touched them.

She fought to keep from puckering and leaving a kiss on that finger.

What was she thinking? It wasn't as if he'd want her to kiss him. He wasn't there to get involved, especially with a grieving widow. Harm was there to relax and enjoy his vacation.

Yet Talia couldn't deny those female parts that had been dormant since her husband's death had come alive when Harm had touched her. How, after only a year, could she be interested in another man? Knowing what it was like to lose the love of her life, she wasn't ready, nor was she certain she could handle the potential heartache again.

She'd been blessed with true love with a kind, gentle man who saw the beauty of the earth and shared it through his photography. Talia wasn't at all sure she could love anyone else. And Harm was completely different. He had harder edges and deeper scars. He wasn't anything like Michael.

But those hard edges called to her, making her want to smooth them. When he touched her with his callused hands, she could imagine those hands skimming over her naked skin, bringing her body back to life when she thought it wasn't possible.

Talia stepped back. "Thank you," she said. Not sure whether she was thanking him for checking the room or for reminding her that she was still alive, a woman who had a body that required more than just food and sleep.

Harm faced her. "You'll wait here?"

She nodded.

As soon as he turned his back and entered the room, she pressed her palms to her heated cheeks.

Get a grip, woman, she chastised herself. *He's off-limits. You're not ready.*

You loved Michael.

Her last thought brought her back to earth with a thud. She'd loved her husband. Past tense. Michael was gone. But he wasn't forgotten.

Harm was back far too soon. "All clear."

"Good." Talia forced a smile and stepped through the doorway, past Harm and into the bedroom. After a cursory glance to make certain everything was clean and in order, she joined Harm in the hallway and led him to the room he'd sleep in. If it was the one closest to hers, she couldn't let that bother her. It wasn't as though she'd picked it intentionally. The room just happened to be available, with clean sheets and a fully equipped bathroom.

So why didn't you put Big Jake in it?

Talia shrugged off the nagging thought and waited until Harm emerged with the all-clear announcement.

"This will be your room, if you don't want to stay in the cabin."

"I'll grab my gear and move in tonight." He looked around the hallway. "Where do you stay?"

Talia hesitated.

"It's okay," he said with a slight smile. "I'm not

going to put the moves on you. I just want to know which way to run if I hear a scream in the night."

"I'm not worried about that," she said. "I sleep with a pistol under my pillow."

Harm's eyebrows rose. "And I bet you know how to use it."

She nodded. "With deadly accuracy. My husband taught me how. I practice enough to be good at it. A lone female in the African bush is a natural target. Even when my husband was alive, I was alone quite often when he took groups on camera safaris."

"I'm glad to hear it. I really am surprised that you haven't moved back to the States by now."

She glanced away. "I don't have anyone back in the States. My parents died in a car crash shortly after I married Michael. It was part of the reason I didn't mind moving to far-flung places. I didn't have a home to fall back on. The world was our playground. I followed him around for the first few years of our marriage. Then we bought this place and built it up to what it is today. I couldn't just walk away when he died."

"I get it. I don't have family back in the States. Just my brothers."

"You don't have family, but you have brothers?" Talia frowned. "I don't understand."

Harm's chest swelled with the pride of belonging. "My teammates are my brothers. I'd do anything for them."

"And they'd do anything for you," Talia added.

"I know families with real brothers who aren't as close," Harm said. "I didn't understand the brotherhood until I became a SEAL. When the going gets tough, I know they have my back, and I have theirs."

In that moment, Talia envied Harm. When Michael was alive, she could rely on him to be there for her. But he'd died, leaving her without a support system. Yes, she had the staff of the resort, but they had their families, and lately, they were skittish and scared of coming to work.

"I'll tell you what," Harm said. "While I'm here, I'll have your back. You need something, I'm your man."

"Thanks," Talia said. "Again, I don't want to rely on anyone. You and your team are only here for a week. Then you'll be gone. Besides, I've dealt with rumblings before."

"What do you mean?"

"A while back, the local witch doctor stirred up my staff and the community. Ever since Michael died, Raila Gakuru has been campaigning against the All Things Wild resort, spreading rumors and innuendos. He started out whispering that the area would have very bad luck—bad juju—as long as the resort was run by a woman."

Harm's jaw tightened. "Nice guy."

"For the past year, when bad things happened, Gakuru attributed it to me. I ignored the claims, hoping the rumors would die down. And, for the most part, they had. Until a few weeks ago, when the poachers showed up stealing baby animals for sale to foreign markets." She smiled. "Thankfully, you and your team were here to thwart their efforts."

"Seems we didn't stop all of it."

Talia crossed the hallway to a linen closet, extracted two bath towels and turned. "My gut tells me this is totally different from the poachers who were stealing animals. I think someone is trying to scare me off."

"The witch doctor?"

"Maybe."

"I could have a talk with him, if you like."

She shook her head. "No. That only gives him more credibility. Ignoring him worked the first time. I'm leaning toward repeating that tactic, since it worked before."

Harm shrugged. "Seems like it didn't work well enough, if he's back at it."

Talia entered the bedroom and laid the towels on the end of the bed, then straightened. "Either way, it's not your problem. It's mine and I'll handle it. You're a guest." She gave him a lopsided smile and moved past him, back out into the hallway. "Enjoy your stay."

Harm threw a snappy salute. "Yes, ma'am."

She grinned. "That's more like it. Now, let me get back down to my kitchen and see if any of your friends want to move to the lodge." She headed toward the stairs only to be brought up short by a hand on her arm.

"If someone is trying to scare you away, you could be in danger."

"I have my gun," she reminded him, her arm tingling where he held it.

"Are you a good enough shot to kill a cobra in your bed?"

She nodded. "I'm that good." At least she hoped she was. But she wouldn't let him know she wasn't quite so sure.

Harm held her gaze for a long moment, his hand tight on her arm. "What if whoever is playing these games gets more personal?"

Talia lifted her chin, her entire body tingling now. Why couldn't he let go of her and sever the electric current racing along her nerve endings? "What do you mean, more personal?" she asked, her voice breathy. She cleared her throat and continued. "I'd say attacking my clients is already pretty personal."

"What if someone corners you?" He backed her against the wall. "Are you prepared to fight for your life? Do you know how to defend yourself?"

Her body hummed with the electricity burning through her nerves and veins. "I think I can," she whispered, her gaze shifting to Harm's lips. Holy hell, she had the sudden urge to kiss them. What was wrong with her?

Harm shook his head. "There is a difference between thinking and knowing." He bent close. "I can show you some moves."

She ran her tongue over her suddenly dry lips.

"I'm sure you can…" Sweet heaven, she was sure he had some sexy moves. And now wasn't the time to demonstrate. Not when she was steps away from the room she'd shared with her dead husband.

"I… I have to go now." Talia pushed her arms between them and raised them sharply, knocking his hands from where they gripped her shoulders. Then she ducked beneath them and made a dash for the stairs.

A warm chuckle followed her down the staircase, making her insides hot and feeling like liquid. She'd do well to stay away from the handsome SEAL. Harm could rock her world. And she wasn't ready for her world to be rocked. Though Talia suspected he was halfway there, and it scared the bejesus out of her.

Chapter Three

While Talia was in the kitchen helping his teammates feed their late-night hunger, Harm stepped out of the lodge and hurried to the cabin he'd been assigned, wishing he had a flashlight to shine at the ground. Though he didn't have a deadly fear of snakes, the cobra in Big Jake's bed would shake him as much as it had shaken his friend.

Once he reached the cabin, he flipped on the light switch and made a careful study of the interior, just in case another cobra had found its way in while Harm had been away.

The question burning in his mind was how did a cobra get inside Big Jake's cabin? And why would it end up on the bed?

After a thorough search of his own cabin, Harm studied the bed. The comforter had been neatly fitted over the entire bed with a colorful throw draped at the foot. Someone could have stashed the snake in the throw. Until Big Jake slid beneath the comforter, the snake might not have felt the need to move.

Using a hanger, Harm lifted the throw off the end of the bed. Nothing lay beneath. He shook the fabric. Nothing fell from the folds. Harm released the breath he'd been holding and set his gear bag on the bed. He unearthed the flashlight he kept in an outside pocket of the bag and unzipped the main opening.

A few minutes later, he'd ascertained his bag was free of snakes, bugs or anything else that might keep him up at night. After he zipped the bag, he hefted it onto one shoulder and left the cabin, closing the door behind him.

The screaming howl of jackals filled the night. Harm didn't consider himself very superstitious, but Africa and the savanna lent itself to being creepy.

He hurried back to the lodge and up the stairs to ditch his bag before joining the rest of the gang in the kitchen.

His five teammates were seated at a large wood and steel kitchen table, digging into ham sandwiches and drinking beer.

"Would you care for a sandwich?" Talia asked.

T-Mac held up what was left of his. "You gotta try the ham. I don't know what the chef put on it, but it's damned good." T-Mac glanced at Talia. "Sorry. Didn't mean to curse."

She smiled. "No worries. I've heard worse. I think I've even said worse."

Harm's heart contracted at Talia's sweet smile. Curse words from her mouth wouldn't detract one bit from her beauty. Not wanting to leave the kitchen yet, he tipped his head toward the container of ham slices. "I'd like a sandwich, but I can make it myself."

"No need. Sit with your friends," she ordered. "It won't take me a minute."

"At least let me help." Harm washed his hands in the sink and returned to pull lettuce off a head on the counter.

Talia laid bread on the counter. "Mustard or mayo?"

"Both," Harm replied.

She spread mustard on one piece of bread and layered ham slices over it.

Harm laid the lettuce on the ham, while Talia slathered mayonnaise onto the other slice of bread. She laid it on top of the pile of ham and held it from falling off to the side. "Could you hand me the knife?"

Harm reached around her, his chest brushing against her back.

Talia stiffened, her hand freezing on the sandwich.

"I'll cut that," he said.

She held the sandwich with one hand.

Harm's arm curved around her, and he held the knife over the bread. About that time, he caught a whiff of her perfume and couldn't think past wanting to get closer to identify the scent.

"Are you going to cut it?" she whispered.

Entirely too aware of his hostess, Harm pressed

the handle of the knife into her palm. "Maybe it would be best if you did the honors."

She nodded. "Right." Her hand shook as she sliced through the bread, ham and lettuce. With quick efficiency, she laid the two sides of the sandwich on a plate and poured potato chips beside it. "Here you go." Talia shoved the plate toward Harm. "You can help yourself to the drinks in the refrigerator. If you prefer tea or coffee, I'll make some for you."

"Thank you. I'll have a beer, but I can get it myself." He took the plate from her hands, his fingers brushing against hers, sending an electrical current up his arm and all the way down to his groin.

Talia snatched her hands away and tucked them into the back pockets of her jeans. By the way she was acting, she might have had a similar reaction to his touch.

A smile tugged at the corners of his lips as he carried the plate to the table. He liked that he unnerved her as much as she did him.

Diesel reached out as if to snag Harm's sandwich.

"Touch it and I'll break your fingers," Harm warned. That sandwich meant more than something to fill his belly. Talia had helped make it. For him.

The other SEAL held up his hands in surrender. "Just kidding with you. I kind of like my fingers the way they are. Need them to shoot."

"You know better, Diesel. No one comes between a SEAL and his sandwich," Pitbull said. As if to prove his point, he stuffed the last bite of his sandwich into his mouth and grinned like a chipmunk with his cheeks full of nuts.

Big Jake stood, carried his plate to the sink and stopped at the refrigerator on the way back. He snagged two longneck bottles of beer and handed one to Harm. "Didn't think you'd want to leave your food unattended with these vultures around."

"You got that right." Harm shot a narrow-eyed glare at the others sitting at the table and then gave a chin lift to Big Jake. "Thanks, man."

"You're welcome." He patted his flat stomach and stretched. "I think I'll be hitting the rack."

"I'll show you the room," Talia offered.

Big Jake grabbed his duffel bag and followed Talia out of the kitchen.

Harm couldn't focus on his food until Talia had left the room. His pulse hadn't slowed since he'd touched her hand.

"I'm going to marry that woman," T-Mac said.

Harm's gaze shot to his teammate, and he nearly crushed his sandwich in his fist. "Why do you say that?"

T-Mac laughed. "Seriously?" He tipped his head toward the door Talia had disappeared through. "She makes a mean ham sandwich, she's beautiful, and most of all, she's not afraid of snakes."

Dr. Vega set her bottle of water on the table, a frown wrinkling her pretty brow. "And you think those are enough reasons to marry someone?"

"It's enough in my book," T-Mac said.

"You barely know the woman," Pitbull said.

"And how long have you known Marly?" T-Mac raised his eyebrows and smiled at Marly. "No offense, Marly."

She shook her head, her sandy blond hair swinging around her chin. "None taken."

Pitbull lifted Marly's hand. "We're different. There was a connection between us from the start."

Marly lifted his knuckles to her lips and pressed a kiss to them. "Well, not from the start, but shortly after. I was more interested in making him sweat in the copilot's seat of my airplane."

"And I did," Pitbull said.

"Yes, but you held strong." Marly smiled into his eyes. "Even when you were scared out of your mind."

Pitbull frowned. "I wasn't scared out of my mind."

"Uh-huh." Marly pressed his hand to her cheek. "Even when we landed in the middle of a herd of zebras?"

"Crash-landed," he corrected.

"I prefer to call it a controlled emergency landing." Marly lifted her chin. "I was in control the entire time."

"Yes, you were," Pitbull said and leaned across to kiss her lips.

Harm watched their public display of affection and found himself wishing he had that kind of relationship with a woman. His thoughts immediately went to Talia and quickly switched back to T-Mac.

He'd be damned if his teammate stole Talia's heart

out from under him. Not that he held her heart. She'd loved her husband.

The tension ebbed from Harm's body. T-Mac didn't have a chance with Talia. For that matter, neither did Harm. It would take a very special man to win her heart after the love she'd shared with her husband. Harm wasn't sure he, T-Mac or anyone else on his team was that special. He loved them like brothers, but none of them were as creative or sensitive to the plight of the animals on the savanna. Yeah, they cared about their existence, but not to the point where they'd choose to give up their lives in the States to run a resort in Kenya.

Talia deserved someone strong, yet sensitive and creative, who would love her so very much he'd be willing to risk it all to keep her safe.

Harm bit into his sandwich, thinking about Talia's husband, Michael. Any man who would bring his woman out to the wilds of Africa without a backup plan had to be too focused on his own dreams and desires to think about the needs of the woman he promised to love, honor and cherish. Somewhere in those marriage vows should have been another promise… to protect. By dying, Michael had left his wife exposed to all the dangers inherent to life in Africa. He should have had a plan in place for her should he be injured or killed.

The man obviously didn't love her enough, or he would have left instructions on what to do in the event of his death.

Talia was a lone woman in a country where she didn't have family or a support system. And from the sound of it, the local witch doctor was using her femininity against her and turning the community against her as well.

"T-Mac, you need to focus on women within your reach," Pitbull said. "Talia lives in Africa. What kind of relationship could you have if she's half a world away from you ninety-nine percent of the time?"

T-Mac shrugged. "Love will find a way. I mean, look at you and Marly. All she had to do was blow up her airplane and voilà!" He waved his arm to the side. "She's moving to the States."

"Let me get this straight," Harm said. "Are you planning on blowing up the resort? Because if that's your plan, you'll have to go through me to do it."

"Well, no, but my point is, things have a way of working out." T-Mac frowned. "You don't have to take me literally." He stared across the table at Harm, his eyes narrowing. "Wait. What does this mean? Do you have feelings for our pretty hostess?" His eyes widened and a smile spread across his face.

Harm's brow dipped. "I didn't say that. I'm just saying she's got enough problems without worrying about one of her guests destroying her livelihood."

T-Mac's grin broadened. "You like her." He glanced around at the faces of the other four men in the kitchen. "The most confirmed bachelor of all of us has a thing for Talia." He whooped. "Hot damn.

This ought to be fun to watch. The harder they are, the bigger the fall."

"I thought it was the bigger they are…" Marly commented. "And what do you mean, Harm's the most confirmed bachelor? I thought you were all pretty happy being single."

"I thought we were, too," Pitbull said. "Then Diesel met Reese, I fell for you, and Buck reunited with Dr. Vega. Apparently, even the most confirmed bachelors are susceptible to falling in love."

Harm shook his head. "Not me."

T-Mac laughed. "I'd be willing to give up my pursuit of the beautiful Ms. Talia to see the cynical Harmon Payne fall to the greater power of love."

Harm frowned at T-Mac. "Yeah, well, it isn't going to happen. You know as well as I do that we're not cut out for relationships. Not in our line of work." He cast a quick glance at Dr. Vega and Marly. "No offense. You might be the exceptions. Although what you see in Pitbull and Buck, I'll never figure out."

Thankfully, Marly and Dr. Vega laughed.

"It's finding the right woman who can handle the long separations," Buck said. He took Dr. Vega's hand and smiled down into her eyes. "It takes a very independent woman who is capable of standing on her two feet. I think Talia meets that criteria."

"She's a business owner in a challenging industry and country," Marly pointed out.

"She obviously doesn't need a man to function," Dr. Vega said.

"And neither do either of you two women," T-Mac said.

The ladies nodded.

"But we choose to be with our guys." Marly laid a hand on Pitbull's arm.

"Not because we are dependent on them, but because we want to be with them," Angela Vega said with a smile.

Harm shrugged. "Again, I believe you ladies are the exception."

"Be careful, Harm," Marly warned. "You can't paint all women with the same brush. Many of us are of stronger stock."

Angela studied him with narrowed eyes. "What happened in the past that turned you against relationships? Did you get a Dear John letter that broke your heart? Or am I getting too personal?"

Harm stiffened. The doctor's words hit far too close to home.

"Yeah, Harm, who rocked your love boat?" T-Mac asked.

"That's it." Harm glared at his teammates. "My love life—"

"Or lack thereof," T-Mac inserted.

"—is not up for discussion," Harm continued. "If and when I have a love life, which is highly unlikely, you all will be the last to know."

"I have a feeling we'll know before you," Diesel said. "You'll be in a huge state of denial."

"Like you are now," Buck added.

"Whatever." Harm spun toward the door. "I'm calling it a night." He marched toward the door, ready to get the hell out of the conversation.

"You can run from the truth," T-Mac called out, "but you can't hide."

He was so intent on leaving the kitchen, Harm didn't notice Talia coming from the opposite direction until he plowed right into her.

She bounced off his chest and might have fallen if he hadn't gripped her arms to steady her.

Laughter erupted behind him.

"See? You can run…" T-Mac said.

"I'm sorry. I should have been more careful," Talia said, looking up at him with her clear blue eyes, a smile curving her soft lips.

"No," Harm said, his voice gruff. "My fault. I should have been looking where I was going." His first inclination was to pull her into his arms and crush her to his chest. But the lingering chuckles behind him reminded him of the conversation his teammates had subjected him to.

He wasn't in the market to find love. But if he were, Talia was an amazing woman. Strong, sensitive, loyal and beautiful. Damn. "I can't go there," he muttered and set her to the side.

"What do you mean?" she asked, her eyebrows

forming a V over her nose. "Go where?" She looked past him to the crowd in the kitchen. "Did I miss something?"

T-Mac slapped a hand to his knee and gave a bark of laughter. "Boy, did you."

Harm had no desire to be humiliated in front of their hostess. "Good night." He continued toward the staircase and took the steps two at a time, laughter following him all the way up.

He hoped his teammates wouldn't share their discussion with Talia. He didn't want her to get the wrong impression. He wasn't interested in her. Even if her touch sent fire ripping through his veins and her smile made his knees wobble.

TALIA STOOD IN the doorway of the kitchen, her arms still tingling where Harm had gripped them.

His friends were laughing and grinning like fools. Even Marly and Dr. Vega were smiling.

"I feel like I'm missing out on a joke. Someone want to fill me in?"

T-Mac turned to the others. "Should I?"

"No," Buck said.

Diesel shook his head. "Just leave it."

T-Mac frowned. "You take all the fun out of poking the bear."

Talia stared from T-Mac to Diesel and back. "Bear?"

"Harm." T-Mac raised his hands. "That's all I'm going to say."

"Good," Marly said. "Now, if you'll excuse me, I could use some sleep."

"Me, too." T-Mac pushed back from the table and stood. "After I check for snakes." He carried his plate to the sink.

"You're welcome to stay in the lodge, if it will make you feel better." Talia gathered more plates from the table. "I'll happily make up a room for you and anyone else who wants to move in from the cabins."

"I'll risk the cabin." Buck slipped his arm around Dr. Vega. "If you're willing."

Angela smiled up at him. "As long as you go in first and make sure we don't have a cobra waiting in our bed."

Buck shuddered. "I can't imagine what Big Jake must have felt seeing that snake."

"I would have blown the bed and half the room away trying to kill that cobra," T-Mac said.

"Because you're a lousy shot." Diesel draped an arm over T-Mac's shoulder. "Come on, I'll help you clear your cabin so you can sleep without fear of being snake bit. And so you don't feel the need to put holes in the furniture or walls."

"Thanks, dude," T-Mac said with a twisted grin. "You're a real friend."

"I've got your six, man," Diesel said.

The two men left the kitchen, followed by Buck and Angela and Marly and Pitbull.

Though they poked and prodded each other, they

seemed to be a tight-knit team, willing to do anything for each other.

Eventually, Talia was alone. She cleaned the dishes, dried them and put them away. She knew she was procrastinating, avoiding going to bed. Many nights she'd stayed up into the wee hours of the morning, finally falling asleep in one of the lounge chairs in the common area rather than going up to the room she'd shared with Michael.

A few months after Michael's death, she'd moved her things out of their room and into a smaller room to open up the master suite to guests. She'd told herself it was because she could charge a premium for the larger room. The reality was she didn't want to sleep in the room she had shared with Michael. Too many memories kept her awake at night.

But tonight, she wasn't awake because of her memories of Michael. She didn't want to walk past the room Harm was sleeping in to get to hers. The thought of only a wall standing between them as they lay in their beds seemed too personal. None of her other guests had that effect on her. Why would Harm?

She wrapped her arms around her middle and walked into the common area. Maybe she'd sleep in one of the lounge chairs. She always woke before her guests. In that case, she could be up and dressed for the day well before they came down for breakfast.

Talia sat on one of the long sofas and tucked her legs beneath her.

Wide-awake and wired, sleep wasn't going to come to her at once. The cobra, the poachers and other happenings were getting too close for comfort. Something had to give. Her chef had suggested she hire the local witch doctor to lift the evil spell from the walls, floors and grounds. She hadn't been keen on doing that.

First of all, Talia didn't believe in magic, but the people who worked for her did. Second, the witch doctor could be the one behind all of the shenanigans. He could be setting her up for extortion.

However, if things didn't improve soon, her staff would stop coming to work. She'd have to run the place by herself. She could do it during the slow season, but not when the lodge and all the cabins were full. Someone had to lead the safaris while another person cooked enough to feed the guests, tended to the cabins and maintained the grounds.

No, she couldn't do all those tasks alone. If her staff quit coming to work, she'd have to take fewer and fewer guests. If she couldn't bring in guests, she couldn't pay the bills. She'd be forced to close.

Then what? After Michael was killed by a rhino, she'd automatically assumed she'd continue on with the operation of the resort. Yes, it had been primarily Michael's dream, but while he was alive, she'd shared that dream. After his death, she'd been in such a funk, she couldn't bring herself to consider other options. Michael was buried in Africa. She hadn't wanted to leave.

This place, the lodge, the resort, the savanna, had memories seared into every corner, every tree, everywhere she looked.

Yet her thoughts continued to drift up the stairs to the man in the room beside hers. Guilt rushed over her like a heat wave. Only a year had passed since Michael's death. She shouldn't be feeling anything for anyone other than her husband. Should she?

Talia reached for one of the throw pillows on the cushion beside her and hugged it to her chest. She missed being able to hug someone. Not just a friendly hug, but one that involved body-to-body contact. A real, warm, lasting hug she never wanted to end.

Not like holding a pillow. A pillow couldn't return the sentiment. Someone with thick, strong arms was needed to make that connection. Someone who could return the pressure and make her feel safe and loved. And not so very…alone.

"Why are you sitting down here all alone?" a deep resonant voice asked.

Talia started and glanced up into the warm, deep brown eyes of the man she'd been thinking about.

He wore jeans and a well-worn T-shirt stretched tautly over the broad expanse of his chest. And he was barefoot.

Talia fought the urge to drool like Pavlov's dog. "I…uh…" She gulped hard to keep from squeaking. "…wasn't sleepy."

"Too much excitement?" He nodded toward the cushion beside her. "Mind if I sit?"

Excitement? Oh, yeah. She pretended a nonchalance she didn't feel. "Please. Sit where you like." Inside she fought a losing battle between self-preservation and desire. If he accepted her offer to take the seat beside her on the sofa, self-preservation didn't stand a chance.

Harm dropped onto the cushion inches away from Talia.

Her breath caught and her pulse kicked into high gear.

Sitting half facing her, Harm leaned his elbows on his knees. "The snake in Big Jake's cabin worrying you?"

"For a start," she admitted. No use telling him she was also worried by her feelings for him. He didn't need to know that little bit of information. If she thought witchcraft and bad juju were making her vulnerable, letting a man know he made her weak in the knees would expose her in a way she was nowhere near ready to handle.

Talia prayed he didn't try anything silly, like kissing her. She wasn't sure she had the power to resist.

Chapter Four

Harm had been in his room, listening for the sounds of Talia's footsteps on the landing outside his door. When he hadn't heard them and the lodge had quieted, he'd left his room and descended the stairs, going in search of the pretty hostess.

He'd been surprised to find her sitting alone on a sofa, a pillow clutched to her chest, her blue eyes staring into the distance.

Talia hadn't noticed his barefoot approach.

If he'd been smart, he'd have crept back up the stairs and gone to bed. But he couldn't leave her there. The tug at his heart refused to let him leave. So he'd taken the seat beside her, with no idea what to say or how to comfort a widow.

"Thank you for adjusting the room assignments for us," he said.

She shrugged. "I didn't have to do much. It's not like I have an entire lodge full of guests." She hugged the pillow tighter. "I can't continue to run this place without a staff or paying guests. If things don't turn around soon, I'll be forced to shut the doors, sell the resort and find employment somewhere else."

"Is it that bad?"

She nodded. "The staff thinks I'm the one caus-ing the problems. Because I'm a woman trying to run the place, I'm creating bad juju."

Harm's jaw tightened. "That's a bunch of bull."

"You know that and I know that, but my staff is very superstitious. I wouldn't be surprised if some-one else quits tomorrow when he or she finds out there was a cobra in one of the cabins." Talia drew in a deep breath and let it out on a sigh. "It just makes more work for me. But if I don't have guests, I won't need the staff and I won't have a reason to stay at the resort."

"Have you considered selling?"

Her lips pressed into a thin line. "Even when Mi-chael was alive, I was in charge of the day-to-day running of the lodge and cabins. Michael took care of expeditions, entertainment and nature hikes."

She stared around the room at the photos on the walls of the animals in their natural habitat. "He always came back with the most incredible photo-graphs." Her gaze stopped on Harm. "I took care of everything else. But the lodge and the cabins weren't why the guests came. They came to see what Michael saw. He sold his photographs world-wide. He was well-known for how beautifully he captured the animals and the savanna. The guests came from all over the world to see what had inspired him."

Harm snorted softly. "You didn't answer my question."

Her cheeks blossomed with color, and she glanced down at the pillow. "I'm sorry. What was the question?"

"Have you considered selling the resort?"

She looked away, gnawing at her bottom lip. "I guess most women who'd lost their husbands would have sold something like the resort by now." She glanced back at Harm. "I didn't because I couldn't imagine anything else. What would I do?"

"You could go back to the States where it's less dangerous, for one." He leaned toward her. "You could start over and choose any career you want."

"But I love running the lodge and catering to the guests."

"Even now that your husband is gone?"

Talia's lips twisted. "I don't know."

"You don't know, or you're afraid to say the truth because you'll feel guilty for wanting something different from what Michael had in mind?"

She tossed the pillow aside and leaped to her feet. "It doesn't matter what I want. I have the resort. I'm doing the best I can. I just need to figure out who's behind the threats to me and my guests and take care of it. Life will go on as usual."

"Will it?" Harm stood and reached for her. He knew it was a mistake as soon as his fingers curled around her arms. "Michael's gone, you can't continue to live his dream. What about you, Talia? What do you want?"

She stared up into his eyes, her voice soft… breathy as she said, "I don't know." Her bottom lip trembled and her gaze shifted from his eyes to his mouth.

That moment was Harm's undoing. Talia appeared so vulnerable and confused. He wanted to wipe the concern from her face, to make her lips curl up in a smile. To kiss her.

Before he could think through his next move, he lowered his head and breathed against her lips. "What do you want?"

Her fingers curled into his shirt and she whispered, "You."

Harm claimed her mouth, his lips crashing down on hers. He pushed his tongue past her teeth to sweep the length of hers, caressing, thrusting and demanding a response.

Instead of pushing him away like she should have, Talia raised her arms to lace them behind Harm's neck and pulled him closer.

Harm released her arms and ran his hands down her back, cupped her bottom and pressed her hips to his, his groin tight, swelling with a fresh rush of blood and heat. This was where he'd wanted to be all evening. Holding this woman in his arms, kissing her like there was no tomorrow.

She clung to him, her tongue working against his,

her fingernails digging into the back of his neck, one leg curling around the back of his thigh.

Holy hell, she was hot, sexy and everything Harm had sworn off when he'd received that Dear John letter so long ago. But here he was kissing Talia, completely captivated by the woman and unable to release her.

When the need for oxygen forced him to come up for air, he lifted his head, dragged in a breath and let it go slowly, trying to calm his racing heart.

Talia pressed her forehead to his chest, her hands dropping to curl into his shirt. "What…just happened?"

He chuckled. "I don't know, but I want to do it again."

She shook her head. "No."

Harm's heart stuttered and then tripped all over itself to get going again. "No?" He touched his finger to her chin and tilted her face upward, making her look into his eyes. "Why not?"

"It's not right," she said, her voice catching.

"Why?"

"Michael…" she said, a tear slipping from the corner of her eye.

"Is dead," Harm said softly, not wanting to be insensitive to her loss. "But you aren't."

"Still," she said, her hands flattening against his chest. "I loved him."

"As sensitive a guy as you make him out to be, wouldn't he have wanted you to go on living?"

"I have." She pulled her chin free of his finger and looked away. "Just not like this. He—I wouldn't want you to do it again."

"No?" Harm's arms slipped around her. God, he loved the way she felt against him. "Are you sure you don't want me to kiss you again?"

She tipped her head back and stared into his eyes. "Please," she said, her lips still swollen from making love to his.

He lowered his head until his mouth was only a breath away from hers. "I won't kiss you if you don't want me to. But it seems there were two people involved in that last kiss."

Her breath caught and her body stiffened in his arms. Then she rose upward on her toes, closing the distance between their lips. Talia wrapped her arms around his neck and dragged him even closer until their bodies melded together, almost becoming one. The only way they could be closer would be if they were naked.

Harm clutched her body to him and deepened the kiss, everything else around him fading into a hazy background until the sound of a throat clearing jolted him out of the lusty haze.

Harm lifted his head and stared across the floor at the intruder.

Big Jake stood in his jeans and nothing else. "Sorry, I was just on my way to the kitchen for a glass of water." He hurried by. "Don't mind me. I saw nothing."

Talia pushed away from Harm and smoothed her hands over her shirt and jeans, her cheeks flaming. "I'd better go to my room." She spun and ran for the stairs before Harm could stop her.

Moments later, Big Jake emerged from the kitchen, his lips quirking on the corners. "Confirmed bachelor, eh? Isn't that what you always claimed to be?" He snorted and passed Harm, carrying a glass of milk and a couple of the cookies Talia had offered the group after dinner. "Yeah, right."

"Shut up," Harm grumbled.

"The harder they are, the bigger the fall," Big Jake called out over his shoulder as he ascended the staircase.

As much as Harm wanted to disagree with Big Jake and the rest of his team, he was afraid there was some truth in what they predicted.

TALIA SHOWERED AND combed the tangles out of her hair before slipping into a faded T-shirt and a pair of jersey shorts, her normal sleeping attire. After Michael died, she'd given away all her sexy nightgowns and started wearing old T-shirts and shorts to sleep in. If anyone needed anything, Michael wasn't there to run interference while she dressed. She had to be somewhat presentable at a moment's notice.

But tonight felt different. The soft fabric of the well-worn T-shirt rubbed against her beaded nipples, stimulating them even more. And it all had to do with that kiss.

She crawled into her bed and pulled the comforter up around her, hugging the spare pillow in her arms. It wasn't another person, but the down-filled pillow was all she had. And all she needed, she told herself. Even as the thought crossed her mind, she knew it for what it was…a lie. She needed to be in someone's arms. Otherwise, why had she reacted so strongly to Harm's kiss?

Was a year long enough to mourn the loss of someone you loved? Was it long enough to forget what they'd had together? She shook her head, a single tear sliding down her cheek to plop onto the pillowcase. She'd never forget what she and Michael had. But was that all the love she was allowed to have in one lifetime?

SHE MUST HAVE fallen asleep, because the next thing she knew, someone was knocking on her door. "Mrs. Talia, Mrs. Talia, it's time to wake up."

Talia jerked to a sitting position and stared down at the alarm clock on her nightstand. She'd slept an hour past normal, and she didn't know whether or not she'd have a enough staff to get breakfast for her guests. "I'm up, Nahla. I'll be down in two minutes."

Talia slipped into khaki slacks, a white blouse and her leather hiking boots. Then she pulled her hair back into a sleek ponytail. Makeup-free, she hurried down the stairs to the kitchen.

Nahla was there, helping the rotund chef, Jamba, prepare breakfast and set the table.

"Where's Mshindi and Kamathi? They should be here by now," Talia said.

"Kamathi is out gathering eggs for the breakfast." Jamba shot a glance toward Nahla. "Mshindi isn't coming in."

Nahla reached to place plates from the dishwasher into the cabinet, refusing to meet Talia's gaze.

"Why isn't Mshindi coming in?" Talia asked, knowing the answer but needing to hear it anyway.

"She heard there was a cobra in a guest's room last night. That plus everything else going on has her too scared to come back to work," Jamba said. He set the skillet on the gas stove. "Gakuru performed his magic last night. He says very bad things will happen at the resort as long as a woman runs it."

Talia sighed. "Jamba, do you believe that?"

Jamba shook his head. "No, ma'am. You ran All Things Wild even when Mr. Michael was among the living."

Talia nodded and turned to Nahla. "And you, Nahla? Do you believe the witch doctor Gakuru?"

Nahla fumbled with a glass she'd retrieved from the dishwasher and it fell, shattering against the tile floor.

That was all the answer Talia needed. "Don't move. I'll clean up the glass." She grabbed a broom and a dustpan and scooped up the shards of glass. "Are you that afraid of me?"

Nahla's eyes filled with tears. "No, ma'am. Not afraid of you. But afraid of everything that's happened. I wonder when one of us will be hurt by the bad juju."

Talia couldn't begin to argue with the woman. A cobra in a guest's cabin could just as easily attack a staff member as a guest. Talia took the woman's hands and stared into her eyes. "Do you want to go home?"

The young Kenyan met her gaze, her bottom lip trembling. "Yes, ma'am."

"Then go. I'll take care of the dishes and setting the table."

"But you have to lead the safari today." Nahla shook her head. "I'll stay until you find someone else to fill my position."

Talia shook her head. "At this rate, no one else will come to work for me," Talia said. "Gakuru has the entire village afraid to set foot on the resort."

"That he does, Mrs. Talia," Jamba said.

"It's been a year since Michael died. Why is he so set on scaring me off now?"

Jamba bowed his head, shaking it from side to side. "I don't know, Mrs. Talia. I don't know."

A muffled scream sounded from outside the kitchen door.

Talia started, her gaze swinging toward the sound. "What the he—"

Kamathi burst through the door, her eyes wide in her dark face. "The chickens…" She doubled over, dragging in breaths to fill her lungs. When she could speak again, she faced Talia. "The chickens are all dead."

Talia's heart plummeted into her belly. "What do you mean?" she asked as she hurried toward the door.

"They're dead." Kamathi crossed her hands over her breasts. "The witch doctor was right. This place has very bad juju."

Anger filled Talia. She wanted to tell the woman there was no such thing as bad juju. There were bad people who did bad deeds, but bad juju? No. Instead, she hurried out to the chicken coop to investigate for herself.

What she found made her stomach turn. Inside the fenced-in chicken yard and coop, every last chicken lay dead, ripped to shreds, a bloody mess. As much as she'd like to blame a human for the carnage, a person wouldn't have done this.

"Hey." A large, warm hand descended on her shoulder. "My team will help clean up the mess."

Talia turned and stepped into Harm's arms. Even though she wanted to appear strong, at that moment, all she wanted was to lean on someone.

Harm enveloped her in a hug, pulling her close against his body. "Even from here, I can see paw prints in the dust."

"You can?" Though she'd rather bury her face against his chest, she pushed back enough to stare down at the dusty ground. "Where?"

The navy SEAL squatted on his haunches and pointed at an indention in the loose dust. "Here," he said. "You can see the outlines of the pads of the animal's paws. By the size and shape, I'd guess it was some kind of dog." He motioned toward the tip of the print. "You see the sharper points of the toenails?"

Talia bent closer, studying the imprints. "Couldn't it have been a cat?"

"I don't think so." He stared around at the other prints now clearly visible in the dust. "All of the prints have the toenails. Cats have retractable claws. Some of the prints would have been without toenails."

Talia straightened and walked back to the gate. "But how would a dog have gotten into the chicken yard? The latch on the gate isn't damaged." She glanced around at the fencing. "The fence is intact, and I don't see any holes or damage."

Harm joined her at the gate. "Could someone have left it open?"

Talia shook her head. "I fed the chickens last night and made sure I closed the gate securely. We've had other varmints get into the pen before. My husb— Michael—reinforced the pen and the gate." She shook her head. "I know I closed it tight last night."

"Could someone have come back after you?"

Talia shrugged. "I suppose anyone could have. But why?" She looked up into Harm's eyes. "Why would anyone leave the gate open? These poor chickens…"

Harm slipped an arm around her waist and pulled her against his side. "Whatever killed them didn't stay around to eat. It just killed."

"What a waste." Talia leaned against him, glad to have his strong, solid support. Yeah, she could get through this on her own. Hell, she'd been through worse. But it was nice to have someone there. "I'll have to buy eggs locally until I can get more chickens. Hopefully, I have enough eggs on hand in the kitchen for breakfast."

"Me and the guys are easy. We could eat ham sandwiches again and be perfectly happy." He smiled down at her. "At least it wouldn't be MREs."

Talia laughed, though the effort caught in her throat and lodged there with something that felt like a sob. "Why is this happening to me? You'd think someone was trying to scare me off."

"Given the circumstances, you could be right."

She straightened, her jaw firming. "Well, it's not going to happen. I'm not giving up All Things Wild."

"What we need is to find out who's behind all of the troubles."

"We?" Talia shook her head. "You and your team are guests. You shouldn't have to fight my battles for me. You did it once already when you were here a couple weeks ago. Those poachers could have gotten away with those baby elephants if you hadn't stopped them in their tracks."

"Could the same poachers be back? We stopped their buyers, but that doesn't mean they haven't found new buyers for the animals."

Talia frowned. "It's a constant struggle to protect the animals of the savanna. With so much money to be made in illicit trade of live and dead animals, there aren't enough enforcement personnel to go around. We do what we can by reporting incidents when they happen, but it always seems our efforts are just a drop in the bucket."

"You're doing the right thing. But maybe someone is tired of your doing the right thing."

"Yeah?" Talia sighed. "But who?"

Chapter Five

While Talia worked to calm Kamathi and help the chef prepare breakfast, Harm and his team slipped out to the chicken pen and cleaned up the carnage left by whatever animal had entered. They found one chicken hiding in a tree outside the pen, the lone escapee from the terror of the night before.

Big Jake managed to capture the chicken, much to the delight and ribbing of the rest of the team.

"You can't ignore the irony of Big Jake catching the chicken," Harm said after they'd secured it in the cleaned chicken pen and were on the way back to the lodge.

"How's that?" T-Mac asked.

"They both escaped certain death by a killer animal. It only seems fitting Big Jake caught the chicken and returned it to the relative safety of the pen."

"Didn't look like the pen kept the other chickens safe," Pitbull said, his mouth set in a grim line.

"What about Mr. Wiggins?" T-Mac asked. "Could he have gotten hungry and torn open the gate?"

"Mr. Wiggins was in my room all night," Talia said. "It wasn't the leopard."

"I get the feeling someone opened that gate and left it open on purpose," Diesel said. "I didn't see any sign of forced entry by human or animal."

Harm felt the same. "Question is...who?"

The men continued on in silence. Not one of them had the answer to that question.

In the lodge, the smell of hash brown potatoes, bacon and fried ham slices filled the air.

Harm's belly rumbled despite the unsavory task they'd just performed.

One by one, the men filed into the downstairs bathroom to wash up before entering the dining room, where Talia and her staff had set up a sumptuous buffet of breakfast items.

Talia set a steaming platter of scrambled eggs on the sideboard and turned to face them. "I thought I was going to have to send out a search party for you."

"We had something to do before we could sit down for breakfast," Big Jake said and dusted a feather off his T-shirt.

Talia frowned. "You didn't go clean up my chicken pen, did you?"

The men held up their hands, all innocence.

"Who, us?" Harm shook his head. "I smell bacon." He clapped his hands together and sidestepped Talia to reach for a plate. "Don't let the food get cold."

"Don't take all the bacon," Buck said.

Talia crossed her arms over her chest, her lips

pressed into a thin line. "You shouldn't have done it. You're guests, not staff."

"Done what?" Diesel plucked a crisp piece of bacon off his plate and stuffed it into his mouth.

"By the way," Big Jake leaned close to her and whispered, "you had one survivor. She's safely locked in the pen."

"We nicknamed her Lucky," Pitbull said. "You should have seen Big Jake chasing her around before he caught her."

"We're thinking of changing his call sign to the Chicken Whisperer," Buck said.

Big Jake swung at Buck, clipping his shoulder with a not-so-light tap of his fist. "No, you won't, if you want to live to see thirty."

"I'd risk it," Pitbull said. "Chicken Whisperer has a ring to it."

"Ah, leave the man alone." Marly handed a plate to Pitbull. "Or they'll be calling you Sky Baby or Chicken Little because you always think we're falling out of the sky when we fly."

"Chicken Little thought the sky was falling *on* him, not that he was falling out of the sky." Pitbull leaned over and kissed her on the temple. "Get your fairy tales straight, fly girl."

"My mother didn't read those to me when I was a little girl. I grew up studying books about airplanes." Marly grinned. "My father's influence."

"Any idea what killed the chickens?" Angela Vega asked as she set a plate full of food on the table.

Buck set down his plate and held her chair for her. "Harm seems to think it was canine. Who knew he was a born-again animal tracker?"

"I wonder if it was one of those jackals we heard howling last night." Harm shot a glance at Talia. "Have you ever had trouble with jackals entering your resort area?"

"No," Talia said. "We have had the occasional lion pride wander through, and sometimes the elephants get close. But the jackals always stayed out of sight."

"Did you ask your staff if anyone went into the chicken pen after you last night?"

"I did, but those who are here claim they didn't." She fussed with the items on the buffet, straightening the serving spoons and covering what was left.

Harm placed his plate full of breakfast goodness on the table and waited for Talia to fill her plate and join them.

When she hesitated, he asked, "Aren't you going to have breakfast with us?"

Talia gave him a half smile. "I'm not sure I can eat after seeing all those dead chickens."

"They're all taken care of," Harm said. "We'd like for you to sit with us."

"Yeah, beats looking at Harm's ugly face," Big Jake said.

The other men chuckled.

"Don't wait on me. I'll grab something before we leave for the safari I have scheduled."

"We insist you eat, too," Harm said.

"Yeah, sit," Angela said with a smile. "A safari is an all-day affair, and you'll need your strength to keep up with this motley crew."

Buck gave Angela a teasing frown. "Hey, who are you calling motley?"

"You." She touched his hand. "But I mean it in the nicest way."

"Yeah, yeah." Buck's frown curved upward into a grin. He lifted the doctor's hand and kissed her knuckles. "You're going with this motley crew, aren't you?"

"No, actually, I think I'll spend some time in the village. Nahla said there are a few people who need medical attention and don't have the time or where-withal to get to the nearest clinic."

Buck's frown was back. "I don't know that I like you running around without an escort. I'll go with you."

"I wouldn't hear of you skipping your safari to help me."

"And I'm not going to argue about it. If you go to the village, I go to the village." Buck squeezed her hand.

Angela smiled. "You're a stubborn man, Graham Buckner."

"Damn right I am." He grinned and dug into his food.

"Anyone else backing out?" Talia asked. "I need a head count to know how many sandwiches to pack."

"The rest of us will be going," Pitbull said. "Including Marly. She'll have to fly low today in the back of the safari wagon."

Marly laid down her fork and set her napkin beside her plate. "I'm looking forward to it. I usually only see the herds from over five hundred feet in the air."

"Unless you're crashing into the middle of one," Pitbull reminded her.

Marly gave him the stink eye. "I didn't crash. It was a controlled landing."

"Right. Whatever you say." Pitbull stuffed another piece of bacon in his mouth and grinned while chewing.

Marly rolled her eyes and pushed back from the table. "If you'll excuse me, I'd like to grab a hat and sunscreen before we leave."

"I'm coming." Pitbull jammed another bite of toast into his mouth, grabbed another piece of bacon and stood.

Marly gathered their two plates.

"Don't worry about your dishes," Talia said. "I'll take care of them."

"And lead a safari, and clean the rooms?" Harm stood. "You're amazing, but you can't do it all."

When Talia started to stand, Harm put a hand on her shoulder. "Sit. I'll gather the dishes and get them to the sink. You need to eat. You'll be of no use on the safari if you're passing out from lack of fuel."

"Pushy a little?" she said with a smile and remained seated while Harm, Marly and Pitbull collected the empty plates.

"Touch mine and I'll stab you with my fork," Big Jake said.

Harm chuckled. "I'll let you carry your own plate into the kitchen." He held up his hands. "When you're done, of course."

"Damn right." Big Jake's fierce frown didn't fool anybody. The man liked his food. But it was a standing joke that no one hurried him through his meal. As many meals as he'd missed when on missions, the man deserved to eat at his own pace when on vacation.

Harm, Marly and Pitbull carried the plates to the sink.

"I'll help wash up. You two go get ready for the day," Harm said.

"Going all domestic on us?" Pitbull queried. "Could you iron my boxer shorts for me?"

"Get out or I'll make you dry." Harm popped Pitbull with a dish towel. "Besides, you don't wear boxer shorts."

"Just testing you." Pitbull backed away. "I'm going."

Jamba was busy making ham sandwiches for the day trip. Nahla was nowhere to be seen.

Harm filled the sink with warm soapy water and went to work washing the dishes.

"I have an electric dishwasher, you know," Talia said behind him.

The warmth of her presence filled Harm in a way he'd never experienced before. He liked it when she was around.

"Let me take over. You need to get ready for the safari." Talia slid up next to him and tried to take the washcloth from him.

He held it out of her reach. "If you want to help, you can dry."

She frowned. "You shouldn't be doing my work."

"A few dishes won't kill me," he said. "I might get dishpan hands, but it's a chance I'll take."

Talia laughed and grabbed a dish towel. "You're a very stubborn man."

"I thought that was Pitbull."

"I'm sure you and each of your teammates have a stubborn streak a mile wide, or you wouldn't have made it through BUD/S."

He glanced at her, amazed. "Look at the safari girl knowing about SEAL training."

Her cheeks filled with color. "We have satellite internet here. We're not complete troglodytes." With a shrug she continued, "I have to admit, I did some web surfing after you left the first time."

His heart swelled. "Curious about what we do?"

She took a clean plate from him and ran the cloth over it until it was dry. "I am. I also watched an old DVD of *GI Jane*. Every one of you went through hell to earn the privilege of being a SEAL."

Harm didn't say anything, just dipped his head in acknowledgment and kept washing the plates, cups and flatware until every last item was clean. His time at BUD/S was something he could never forget, nor would he want to. Yes, he'd earned the right to call himself a SEAL, through blood, sweat and more blood and sweat.

Talia kept up with his washing, putting the dishes away as she dried them. When they were finished, the kitchen was clean and their lunches were packed into a sturdy wicker basket.

Harm carried the basket out to the truck wagon. Talia settled it on the floor of the cab on the passenger side. The truck had been rigged with four rows of two seats each in the back and a canvas awning.

The SEAL team gathered around the truck, joking and shoving each other. Harm recognized the raw energy they exuded. It was like this when they were preparing to leave for deployment. On edge and yet keeping it light.

"Are you ready?" Talia asked.

"Yes, ma'am!" the men replied in unison.

Angela and Marly laughed. "We're ready, too," Angela said.

They climbed into the truck. Harm was quick to get in first and took one of the seats closest to the cab. Big Jake took the other.

Marly and Pitbull were next. Diesel and T-Mac claimed the back seats.

Harm knew they'd be packing weapons. He had his nine-millimeter pistol strapped to his calf and his Ka-Bar knife in its scabbard, clipped to his belt.

Pitbull carried a gear bag with his rifle disassembled inside. He could assemble the rifle in five seconds and be ready to take on any threat, be it animal or human. The last time they'd tried to go on safari with Talia, they'd had to fight off a group of poachers attempting to steal baby elephants. They would be even more prepared this time.

Once they were all in place, Talia spoke with the driver and the truck pulled out of the resort compound and onto a gravel road leading into the grasslands.

They bumped along for the first thirty minutes without stirring up more than a few birds. The air had warmed with the rising sun, promising to be a blistering day on the savanna.

Harm was beginning to think it would have been nicer to sit in the cabana with a fan twirling overhead, drinking chilled beer.

The warmth and the steady rocking motion of the truck lurching over potholes lulled Harm into a sleepy state.

He'd just closed his eyes when the truck jerked to a halt.

"What the hell?" Talia said from the front seat. She lifted her binoculars to her eyes and studied the path ahead.

Harm squinted, wishing he had the binoculars to see what Talia was seeing. From where he was, all he could make out was a flock of birds circling over an area of the grassland.

"Go," Talia urged the driver as she lowered her binoculars to her lap.

The driver hesitated. "Are you sure, Mrs. Talia? What if someone is there? Someone with guns?"

"If there are buzzards, there aren't people," she assured him. "We have to know what they're circling."

"Yes, ma'am," the driver said and pulled ahead, picking up speed as they headed for the circling birds.

"What's going on?" Big Jake asked.

"My bet is those birds are circling something dead," Harm said.

Marly and Pitbull leaned over the backs of Big Jake's and Harm's seats.

"Those are some big vultures," Marly said.

"I bet they could carry off a small child," Pitbull agreed.

"Let's hope that's not what they're hovering over."

"It wouldn't be something as small as a child," Talia said. "That many vultures means there's a big meal down below. They're all waiting their turn. Pecking order is strictly enforced."

Harm admired how calm and in control Talia remained in the face of potential danger. Yeah, his team had it right. She was the kind of woman who could handle the rigors of being the wife of a navy SEAL. She could hold her own. Though she'd lost her husband, she continued to operate a posh resort and manage all the staff. Harm could easily fall for a woman with so much grit.

TALIA'S HEART THUNDERED as they neared the spot. The vultures on the ground lifted on long, awkward wingspans and rose into the air. They didn't go far— just far enough to be out of range of the approaching vehicle.

The driver pulled to a halt in front of a large carcass.

"It's a black rhino," Talia said, her jaw tightening. "Damned poachers."

The group dismounted from the truck.

"Based on the smell, I'd say the animal has been dead for at least a day in the heat," Angela said.

Talia nodded toward the dead rhino's head. "They cut off the two horns. Together, they're worth between forty and sixty thousand dollars."

"That much?" Harm asked. "No wonder the poachers are willing to risk their lives doing that."

"Oh, they don't get that much," Talia said. "They might only receive a fraction of that amount, but it's still a heck of a lot more than what they'd earn herding cattle for someone else. The wildlife is being devastated. When these animals are gone…they're gone forever." She took out a satellite phone and punched buttons.

"Who are you calling?" T-Mac asked.

"The local park rangers. They'll want to investigate and see if they can determine who is responsible and where they've gone."

"Will they capture the men?" Diesel asked.

Talia shrugged. "Sometimes they get lucky. But

even if they do capture this bunch, there will be others to take their place. The money is too good, and the middlemen and kingpins are never captured. They'll always be around to lure more men into doing their dirty work."

The dispatcher answered and took down the GPS coordinates Talia supplied, along with the time and date of the discovery. He promised to send out a ranger immediately.

Talia reached into the truck, pulled out a small camera and snapped pictures of the dead animal. Sometimes the rangers took a long time to get out to the carcass. By then, the scavengers could have picked the bones clean, and much of the evidence would have been lost.

She took several pictures before pocketing the camera and turning to her tour group. "I'm sorry you had to see this, but I can't just drive by."

"We wouldn't expect you to," Harm said.

"Now that I've reported to the rangers, we can be on our way. I promised to show you some of the wildlife. Preferably the living, not the deceased. If you'll climb aboard, we can be on our way."

After they loaded into the truck, the driver continued along the dirt road across the savanna, heading deeper into the national preserve.

Soon, they came across a herd of zebras and cape buffalo.

Talia slowed for them to take pictures while she explained how zebras' stripes were like fingerprints, individual and unique to each animal. She also explained how their stripes made it harder for their predators to single one out, confusing them enough to allow them to escape. But as always, the small, weak and infirm were usually the ones to be preyed upon.

An hour later, they stopped beneath the broad branches of an acacia tree, where they were shaded from the harsh noon sun.

Talia pulled out the basket at her feet and distributed the sandwiches to the hungry guests. "You can help yourself to the bottles of water that have been keeping cool in the ice chest on the side of the truck."

Harm grabbed two bottles of water and sat on the ground beside Talia, handing her one. "How are you holding up?"

She tilted her head slightly. "I'm fine. It's the animals of Africa that have it bad. How do we get through to the poachers? They need to understand how bad it is."

"The demand has to be stemmed before the supply dries up," Harm said.

Talia nodded. "In the meantime, we lose thousands of rhinos and elephants to greed each year. At that rate, it won't take long before the animals are extinct."

"You have a big heart, Talia," Harm said.

Talia laughed. "I don't know about that. But I care what happens." She glanced around at the others. "I only hope to share what I know with my guests. It's up to them to take that information back to where they come from and help on a more global scale." Talia could have left when her husband died, but she'd stayed. Partially because this had become all she knew. She had no family back in the States. No one needed her.

But the animals did. Someone had to help them, or they would become extinct.

She glanced toward Harm. "You do understand how important it is to save these animals, don't you?" She waited, praying he was the man she thought he was.

HARM NODDED. "I GET IT. I'll help spread the word. I'll even write my congressman when I get back to civilization and send my dollars to the conservation groups. I'd hate to see these animals wiped off the face of the earth, or be confined to zoos as their only safe haven." Harm finished his sandwich, downed the bottle of water and pushed to his feet. He held out a hand to Talia.

She placed her palm in his and he pulled her up, the spark of electricity tearing through him all over again. The woman made him want so much more than a touch of her hand.

She didn't pull free immediately. Instead, she stared up into his eyes, her own wide, her tongue swiping across her lips.

"Thank you for taking care of the chicken yard this morning."

"It wasn't all me," Harm said. "The guys were more than willing."

"It saved me a lot of time." She tugged at her hand.

Harm released it, albeit reluctantly. He liked holding her hand, but more than that, he wanted to kiss her.

Talia turned to the men. "Thank you for helping with the chickens this morning."

"We should thank you," T-Mac said. "It gave us a new nickname for the Chicken Whisperer."

Big Jake shook his head. "I'll never live that one down."

"Don't worry." Buck clapped a hand to the big guy's back. "We won't let you."

They climbed into the truck and continued on their trek to find more of the wildlife indigenous to the African savanna.

Not long after lunch, they came across a pride of lions lounging in the shade of a baobab tree.

Again, Talia had the driver slow the truck so the guests could take pictures of the animals without getting out. A few minutes after leaving the pride, they came across a group of cheetahs walking along the dirt road coming toward them.

The driver stopped, but the cheetahs kept coming.

Talia laughed. "Don't be alarmed. This group of cheetahs is notorious for visiting the visitors."

Moments later, two cheetahs leaped onto the canvas roof. A third, smaller one jumped onto the seat beside Harm.

Harm moved away as far as possible, hoping the animal was just being curious. "He's not going to rip off my face, is he?"

"I don't think so. *She's* never tried to before," Talia said softly. "Just be very still. Don't make her feel at all threatened."

Harm snorted quietly. "Her...threatened? I think you have that backward."

"Hold that pose, Harm." Big Jake held up his cell phone, snapping picture after picture.

"It's not like I'm going anywhere," Harm said.

The cheetah sniffed at Harm's hand and then his face.

"No, I'm not your lunch," Harm said in a whisper.

The two cats on top of the canvas roof leaped to the ground. The female in the seat with Harm turned and studied the other two.

"That's right. Follow the leaders," Harm said.

In one fluid movement, the cheetah leaped to the ground.

Harm released the breath he hadn't realized he'd been holding.

Big Jake pounded his back. "Wow. That was amazing. I got some great shots. You're gonna love them."

"I'm going to love the fact that the cat didn't rip my face off." Harm scrubbed his hands across his cheeks as if testing to be sure they were still there and intact.

"Well, that was a little tense." Talia laughed nervously. "I can't say that I've ever had big cats jump into the vehicle with my guests."

"Harm loves being a first for things," T-Mac said. "Don't you, Harm?"

"Yeah. I love it," he said, his tone flat.

Talia winked. "You're a good sport, Harm." She looked to the others. "If you're ready, we should be heading back to the resort. The sun will be setting soon," Talia said. "And I have an appointment in the village tonight."

She didn't give him a chance to ask about her appointment. But he would ask before she left the resort that evening. With the way things had been going lately, she'd need an armed escort to see her there and back. He planned on being that escort. What kind of meeting could she have in the village? From what he knew, the village wasn't all that big.

No matter. He'd find out what it was all about and how big the village was. Plus, it would give him an opportunity to question the locals about the poachers. More than likely, one of them knew who they were. Perhaps the poachers would even be at the meeting.

Chapter Six

The sun sat like a blob melting into the horizon as the truck pulled into the resort compound.

Talia was the first person out. She had a lot to do before she could bug out to attend the meeting in the nearby community. She couldn't miss the meeting, as she'd been the one to start the community watch group Women Against Poaching.

In the year since Michael's death, the poaching problem had doubled in size and in disastrous effects. One of the local teenage girls had started working for Talia part-time while she attended the school missionaries had established nearby. Eriku had been a quick study with the tasks Talia had asked her to do. She was good with numbers and even smarter at coming up with graphics for advertising the resort on social media.

As part of her duties, Talia had asked Eriku to research the plight of the African animals. That's when Eriku learned of the impact of poaching on the different species. She'd been so appalled, she'd come to Talia with her concerns. Not content to sit back and do nothing, Eriku had let Talia know she wanted to help.

Together, they'd formed the Women Against Poaching group and had meetings once a month to discuss the progress of educating members of the community. The women had gone out with the intention of helping others, including suspected poachers, to let them know they were being used by the kingpins and middlemen and that once the animals were gone, they'd have nothing. Tourism was the lifeblood of the region. No animals, no tourists, no money. Their people would starve.

That night would be the first meeting after the women had promised to talk to community members and leaders.

It wasn't lost on Talia that the troubles she'd been experiencing had—suspiciously—begun shortly after the formation of the Women Against Poaching group. The poachers had probably gotten word she was in charge. Though she really wasn't. Yes, she'd helped with the education part of it, but Eriku had taken the lead with her friends and neighbors. Her passion and determination were hard to beat.

Talia needed to be there tonight to see how the campaign was going. Women of Kenya had taken more and more leadership roles in the local and national government. Yet, what the group was attempting could have negative repercussions on the females of their society. The men might view them as taking away their only source of income.

Talia gave the SEAL team a tight smile. "I'll see you at dinner. Remember, we're dressing formally tonight, and we could have music and dancing if you'd like."

Harm caught her arm. "Since you have a meeting, let us help you get tasks accomplished."

"Please, that's not how the resort is supposed to work."

"And we don't know how to relax. So, give us something to do or we're likely to cause trouble from boredom." He winked.

"Speak for yourself, Harm," T-Mac said. "I could use a nap before dinner."

Pitbull elbowed the man in the gut. "You can sleep when you're dead." He turned his attention to Talia. "What can we help with?"

"Yes," Marly said. "What can we help with?"

Talia stopped fighting the inevitable and grinned. "Thank you all so very much. I could use a little help. If someone would check out the music and line up what you'd like to listen to, that would be great."

T-Mac held up a hand. "I can do that."

Talia nodded and went on. "Could someone check on the chicken?"

"That would be Big Jake," Diesel said. "On account of he's the Chicken Whisperer."

"Shut up." Big Jake glared at Diesel but smiled at Talia. "I'll feed the chicken."

"I could use a little help setting the table."

Buck and Angela raised their hands. "We can do that."

"I can ice glasses or put the beer on ice," Harm offered.

Talia smiled. "Thank you all. But first, I know we all need showers. I'll meet you in the lodge in thirty minutes. We can take it from there."

Those who were staying in cabins hurried toward their respective units. Big Jake split off to take care of the lone chicken, Lucky.

Harm fell in step beside Talia, making her feel safe and protected. After everything that had happened over the past twenty-four hours, she still hated to admit it, but she liked having the man around. But she couldn't get used to it. He'd leave at the end of the week and she'd have to rely on herself again.

"What is this meeting you're attending tonight?" Harm asked.

"It's an organization I helped found called Women Against Poaching."

Harm grabbed her arm and brought her to a stop. "Are you kidding me?"

She frowned. "No. It's a worthy organization that's trying to stop the poaching by educating the communities as to the impact. One of our local teenagers, Eriku, was so inspired by what she'd learned about poaching from the internet, she wanted to make a difference. I promised to help."

"And when did your troubles start?" Harm asked.

Talia glanced away. "Right after our first meeting a couple weeks ago."

"Holy hell, Talia." Harm shook his head. "Don't you see?"

"That it could be the poachers behind all that's happened?" She nodded. "Yes, it could be the poachers. But I can't stop what has grown into a movement of women. They're doing their best to educate the men, letting them know what will happen if the animals all disappear to the poachers' bullets and machetes."

"You're setting yourself up as a target."

"But I'm not the one going around telling the menfolk they shouldn't kill the animals. Their wives and daughters are doing it."

"Are the men resentful of what the women are doing?" Harm asked.

"They might be. The girls in the village have been attending the missionary school. They're learning so much. Before long, they will be going on to college or university, and after that, they will hold positions of influence."

"If they choose to return to their humble beginnings after being in a city," Harm said, "they might give the menfolk a run for their positions of leadership."

"It might not be quite as easy as that," Talia said. "But I'm glad they're heading in the right direction."

Harm lifted Talia's hand. "In the meantime, the men will know that you had something to do with organizing the group of women. If they have issue with the group, they'll target you, if they haven't already."

Talia nodded. "I understand. But I can't miss the first feedback meeting since we organized and developed our mission."

"All I can think is that you're sitting on a powder keg in a region where poachers sometimes rule communities."

Talia pressed her lips into a tight line. "I realized that, and I expressed my concerns to the girls." She bit down on her lower lip. "That's the main reason I need to be at that meeting tonight—I need to know what we're up against."

"Okay, then. You'll be there." He took her hand and guided her toward the lodge. "And by the way, I'm coming with you."

She opened her mouth to protest but thought better of it. Having Harm along might also give her some clout in the male-dominant society.

Harm held the door for her as she entered the lodge.

"I'm going to check on meal preparation and head up to shower."

"I'll go with you." He grinned. "To the kitchen. And the shower, if you want me to." He winked.

Talia's heart skipped several beats and then thundered against her ribs.

Harm smiled down at her. "I'm kidding and just trying to be helpful." He lifted her hand to his lips.

"But when you're ready, you let me know. I'll be there."

"How? You won't even be in the same country," she whispered.

"I'll find a way," he said, his gaze locking with hers for a long moment. "But for now, let's check on dinner. I could eat an entire side of beef."

Talia laughed, though the sound that came out was more a hysterical giggle. She had loved Michael with all of her heart. How could she be entertaining thoughts of showering with this stranger she barely knew?

HARM FOLLOWED TALIA into the kitchen.

Jamba was working over the stove. Alone.

"Where's Nahla?" Talia asked.

"She left after you did this morning," Jamba said.

Harm's gut tightened. He was sure that news wasn't good for Talia.

"Damn," Talia muttered under her breath. "And Kamathi?"

"Same." Jamba's mouth formed a straight, tight line.

"You've been here working all day on your own?" Talia asked.

Jamba nodded. "Eriku came by after school and made beds and replaced towels."

"Thank goodness." Talia touched a hand to the chef's arm. "Thank you for staying, Jamba."

The older man nodded. "I am not as buried in

superstition as others of the village. While you are at the meeting tonight, you might see some of the others."

"I hope to speak with them and reassure them it's safe to come back to work at the resort," Talia said.

"Don't expect them to return until the witch doctor deems All Things Wild clear of bad juju," the chef warned her.

Talia snorted. "And when will that be? Is he asking for a donation to help resolve the bad karma?"

"He hasn't mentioned a price to cure the resort." Jamba snorted. "But if you offer, I'm sure he'll take your money."

Harm stood back while Talia and Jamba conversed.

Jamba frowned. "Do you want me to go with you to the meeting? You shouldn't go alone." The chef seemed loyal and concerned for Talia's safety.

Harm had to admire the man for wanting to take care of Talia. But while Harm was there, he would fill that need to protect her. "I'll go with her tonight," Harm said.

Talia frowned. "There's no need for either one of you to take me. I can get there and back by myself." She raised a hand. "I don't want to argue about this. You've both done enough."

Harm met Jamba's dark gaze and nodded. "We won't argue. But I'm coming. It will give me a chance to ask questions of some of the villagers about who the cobra handlers are among them, and who are the people with trained dogs."

"You think you'll find the saboteur among the villagers?"

"Doesn't hurt to try," Harm pointed out. "They could be acting under instruction from the poachers. We entered a village in Afghanistan where the women and children had been threatened by the Taliban. They were so fearful, they were ready to take a bullet from us rather than have the Taliban slit their throats in the night."

"That's awful."

It had been awful. He'd had to shoot a woman and her child running toward them, loaded with vests full of explosives. He still had nightmares from it. Yet, had he hesitated, he and his team wouldn't be alive today.

"It might be a boring meeting," Talia warned.

"We can only hope it's boring," Harm said.

Talia nodded. "Jamba, if you have everything under control for the moment, I'll run upstairs for a shower. I'll be down in time to set the table and make a tray of cheese and crackers for an appetizer."

"Take your time. Dinner won't be ready for another forty-five minutes," the chef said.

Harm and Talia left the kitchen and climbed the staircase to the second floor. All the while, Harm remained completely aware of Talia's every move, from the sway of her hips to the way she pushed stray strands of hair back behind her ears. He would have followed her into her room, closed the door and kissed her until she begged for more, but he still wasn't sure where he stood with her. He could sense mutual attraction, but she didn't seem ready to get into another relationship so soon after her husband's death.

And Harm wasn't sure he wanted to start something that would only end when he left. He stopped at his door and rested his hand on the doorknob. "I'll be in the kitchen when you're ready."

"Thank you," Talia said and scurried past him to the next door along the hallway. "Thank you, again, for all you've done for me."

"I haven't done much. No need for thanks."

She smiled. "We may have to agree to disagree. I'll see you in a few." With that parting comment, she went into her room and closed the door between them.

Harm twisted the doorknob and entered his room. Knowing Talia was only feet away on the other side of the wall made his heart beat faster. She'd be stripping out of her dusty clothes and getting into the shower, where water would run over her naked skin.

Harm groaned, his groin tightening with his lusty thoughts. What he needed was a cold shower and some clean clothes. With efficiency born of practice, he stripped, showered and dressed in his nicest black slacks, a button-down white shirt and the tie he'd purchased at the post exchange in Djibouti for the first time they'd been to All Things Wild. Talia had made it clear that dinner was formal. She'd even helped Marly find a dress to wear on two separate occasions when they were there before.

Harm was certain Marly had never worn a formal dress before in her life, but she'd come down dressed to kill. But Talia could outshine any woman in the room, with her rich black hair and her sexy curves. But more than her stunning body, it was her laughter, the smile and the light shining from her eyes that made her so attractive.

After wiping the dust off his dress shoes and strapping his pistol to his calf beneath his pants, Harm straightened his tie and exited the room. He could still hear the shower going in the room next to him. If he hurried, he could get ahead of Talia and do whatever needed to be done before she came down. He found himself wanting to relieve some of her burden. Being down several staff members made it hard for her to keep up. And she'd spent the entire day entertaining them on the savanna, away from the resort that still needed work.

Back in the kitchen, Harm asked Jamba, "What can I do that would help Talia the most?"

"All of the plates, cutlery and napkins are on the table. You could start there."

"We volunteered to set the table," Angela said behind him.

Harm turned to see her and Buck scrubbed and dressed for the evening. Angela wore a long white dress with narrow straps on her shoulders. Her wet hair had been pulled back into a tight bun at the base of her skull.

Buck wore dark slacks, a black button-down shirt and a bright red tie. The contrast of him all in black with Angela's all-white outfit was striking.

Harm grinned. "I feel like I'm staring at the angel and the bad man."

Angela laughed. "We didn't plan it that way, but I kind of like it." She tugged on Buck's tie to straighten it and leaned up on her toes to kiss him. "He makes a great bad man."

"The settings are on the table, ready for you," Harm said.

Buck clapped his hands together. "We're on it."

"There are several types of cheese in the refrigerator," Jamba said. "And the crackers are in the boxes in the pantry." He set a serving platter on the counter. "Cut up the cheese and arrange it on the platter with the crackers."

Harm was just placing the crackers around the cheese when Talia entered the kitchen. She'd pulled her damp black hair up into a loose bun on her crown, exposing the length of her neck.

Harm had the sudden urge to trail kisses down to the base of her throat where her pulse beat rapidly.

"Oh, thank you." She smiled and glanced around the kitchen at the steaming platters piled with steak, baked potatoes and a variety of vegetables. "Is there anything I can do?"

"Ice the glasses, since these are Americans we're serving and they like their ice." Jamba chuckled and shook his head. "I'll never understand why Americans always want to water down their drinks with ice."

"I wouldn't do too many iced glasses. The guys will want cold beer if you have it." Harm twisted his lips. "No ice."

Talia laughed and checked the refrigerator, counting the beer bottles. "Should have enough cold ones for the evening."

Moments later, the rest of the team arrived, raiding the refrigerator for the beer. Soon, they were all seated around the table digging into the platters of food Jamba provided.

Harm sat beside Talia, aware of the warmth of her thigh brushing against him every time she moved.

He downed the amazing steak, half of his potato and a heaping helping of brussels sprouts.

"You like those things?" T-Mac grimaced. "My mother tried to get me to eat those when I was a kid. I swore I'd never touch another when I got old enough to make my own choices."

With a chuckle, Harm popped one into his mouth and chewed. "My grandmother served these at the Thanksgiving table. I don't think I liked them at first, but I eat them now because they remind me of my grandmother."

T-Mac shook his head. "Nope. Not a good enough excuse to eat mini cabbages. Not for me, anyway."

"You were close to your grandmother?" Talia asked.

"She raised me when my parents decided traveling was more important than spending time with their kid."

"I'm sorry."

"About what?" Harm pushed one of the morsels around on his plate. "My grandparents lived on a small farm in south Texas. They were retired, so they took me to all my school and sporting events. And we went to the beach a lot during the summer."

"What made you want to join the navy?" Talia asked.

"Yeah, Harm, why did you join the navy?" Big Jake echoed.

"I saw a recruiting video about the Navy SEALs," Harm answered and ate another brussels sprout.

"That's it?" Big Jake frowned. "You weren't trying to prove anything to your parents, a friend or a woman?"

Harm shook his head. "No. I liked challenges. I set records for my high school on the track team and swim team, and I lifted weights. I thought I'd give it a shot. I was pretty sure I could make it through the training."

"And you did." Big Jake clapped a hand against his back. "Like we all did."

"Yeah. I got recycled and almost didn't make it through," Harm said.

"That's right. You got sick or something," Pitbull said. "I remember you telling me about that. In the middle of Hell Week."

"I would have stayed the course, but the docs pulled me."

"Wow, I can't imagine doing Hell Week twice. I'm not sure I could have done that."

"Yeah, well, by then you know what you're capable of and that it will end eventually. You just have to make it to lunch, then dinner, then breakfast the next morning until you get all the way through."

"That's how I survived BUD/S," Diesel said. "One minute, one hour, one day at a time. I lived in the moment, telling myself it wouldn't last forever."

The other members of the team nodded solemnly.

"Well, we're all glad you made it." Marly glanced around at the people at the table. "Otherwise, we wouldn't be where we are today. I might have been sold to the highest bidder in a sex trade business."

"And I might have been captured by a Sudanese tyrant," Angela added. "And who knows what would have happened to me?"

"And Reese could have died in the jungle when she was kidnapped and taken to the Congo," Diesel said.

"Have I said thank you for choosing All Things Wild for your vacation? You guys have helped me in more ways than I can ever repay you for. The last time you were here, you helped find and bring down the poacher stealing baby animals. I couldn't have done it."

"Don't underestimate yourself," Harm said. "By reporting what you find, you help the rangers keep tabs on poaching activities."

"Maybe so, but it doesn't stop them," Talia argued. "I think some of them are in cahoots with the poachers or their middlemen." She pushed back from the table. "I'm sorry to duck out on you, but I have a meeting to go to in the village. T-Mac will make sure there is music, and you're welcome to push the furniture around in the great room for dancing. Help yourself to the liquor in the lounge. Basically, make yourself at home. I'll be back later."

"You're not going by yourself, are you?" Big Jake said. "What happened to your hired guards?"

Talia grimaced. "I had a hard time hiring guards after two were killed the last time you guys were here. With the witch doctor stirring up rumors, it's impossible to get anyone to help at the resort."

"But don't worry, Talia's not going alone," Harm said. "I'm going with her."

"Do you need more of us to escort you?" Big Jake asked.

Talia shook her head. "I don't anticipate any problems. Having Harm with me will be more of a bonus than a necessity." She smiled. "Thanks anyway. I'm sure you all are tired from the day in the field."

"Ha," Buck said. "That was a walk in the park

compared to what we're used to. I could use a little exercise." He grinned at Angela. "Feel like cutting the rug with this salty dog?"

The doctor smiled up into Buck's eyes. "It's been a long time since you've taken me dancing."

"Then let me remedy my failings." Buck stood and held Angela's chair for her. "Madam, would you honor me with a dance?"

"I'd love it." Angela took the man's arm and let him lead her from the room.

T-Mac scrambled to his feet and grabbed a dinner roll from the basket on the table. "Let me get the jukebox going."

"Pitbull and I will clear the table," Marly said.

"You can leave the dishes," Talia insisted. "I'll take care of them when I get back."

"No worries," Marly said. "Just go, or you'll be late."

Harm hooked his hand through Talia's elbow and led her toward the front door.

Talia grabbed the keys for the safari truck from a hook on the wall and smiled up at Harm. "Thank you for going with me, but you really don't need to."

"I'll let you drive, since you know where you're going." And it would keep his hands free in case he needed to draw his weapon.

Chapter Seven

Darkness had settled in and all the stars in the sky were shining brightly, illuminating the dirt road leading away from the resort.

Harm kept a close watch on the road ahead, looking for movement from the sides as well. With as many wild animals as there were on the savanna, he wouldn't be surprised if they ran across a herd of something...cape buffalo, wildebeests, zebras or impala. And at night, many of the big cats roamed, searching for prey. Ranchers also ran their cattle on the grasslands bordering the preserves.

The village was a collection of huts and shacks made of mud and stick with thatched roofs. Some were constructed of sheets of plywood and tin. At the center of the village, someone had built a fire. Women had gathered around the fire, sitting cross-legged, apparently waiting for Talia's arrival.

When Talia pulled into the village and parked several yards away from the gathering, small children ran up to the truck, calling out her name. "Mrs. Talia! Mrs. Talia!"

Talia stepped down from the vehicle and bent to hug each child and say something nice to them.

"My, you have grown since last I saw you!" she said to the smallest boy.

He grinned and exclaimed, "I can count. Wanna hear?"

"Of course I do." Still squatting in front of him, she nodded. "Go ahead."

The little boy held up one finger. "One." He worked his chubby fingers until he had two up and the others still curled together. "Two." Another finger flexed upward. "Three." Then he grinned, a white flash of baby teeth.

"That was so good." Talia hugged the little boy.

Harm's heart tightened in his chest. He couldn't help thinking that this woman would make a great mother to her own children.

Talia straightened and glanced around the gathering. She strode to one of the women standing near the fire. "Have you seen Eriku?"

The woman nodded and pointed toward the far end of the glowing fire.

A young woman with a head full of tight braids smiled and raised her hand. She made her way through the throng, carefully stepping over those seated on the ground.

When she finally reached Talia, she laughed and hugged her. "I didn't want to start without you."

"You didn't have to wait on me," Talia assured her.

Eriku shrugged. "You are much better at public speaking."

"Only because I've been doing it longer than you."

"Whatever the reason, you're much more convincing than I am. They will listen to you."

Talia touched the young woman's arm and smiled into her yes. "You just have to remember why you're here, and what good you can do by standing up for what's right."

"Yes, ma'am." She stared toward the women seated around the fire. "But there have been problems," Eriku said softly.

"Problems?" Talia asked, her brows drawing together.

Harm leaned closer to hear what the girl was saying.

"Some of the men didn't want to hear what the women had to say." Eriku led Talia over to a woman who sat huddled on the edge of the group, a bright red scarf wrapped around her head and part of her face.

Eriku squatted next to her. "Show Mrs. Talia," she commanded.

The woman slowly lowered the scarf, displaying a dark purple bruise on her right cheek. Her right eye was swollen shut.

Talia gasped. "Who did this?"

The woman shook her head and drew the scarf back up over her face.

"It's bad juju, Mrs. Talia," another woman said. "Gakuru said it's so. He said if we continue to behave as we have, we will be struck barren and our children will become sick."

"It's true," another woman whispered. "My boy is sick. All because I spoke to one of the tribal leaders about the poaching."

"Talking won't make your children sick," Talia said. "The witch doctor is trying to scare you silent."

"We are afraid for our children." A tall, thin woman walked out of the shadows, carrying a baby on her hip. "We can't continue to educate our men and risk our children in the process."

"No, we can't risk our families," Eriku said. "But if we do *nothing*, the animals will die. Without the animals, we will have no tourism. Without tourism, we have no way to buy food to feed our families. We will die of starvation."

The woman with the baby on her hip raised her chin and stared down her nose at the shorter Eriku. "If we do *anything*, our families will die. The poachers will kill us. If not them, the bad juju will poison our water and kill our crops and livestock."

Eriku stared at the woman for a moment longer. "We can't let things continue as they are. We have a responsibility as humans to save our environment, to protect the animals and the land they live on."

"When we can protect our children without fear of attack by poachers, we will work on protecting the animals. Until then, we can't."

The woman with the bright red scarf pushed to her feet. "I am done here."

"As are we," another woman said. She was surrounded by several more women, some gathering children around them.

They moved toward the huts, leaving only a few women left standing near the fire.

The sound of vehicle engines filled the night, and suddenly headlights glared from one end of the road, running through the village.

"Run!" Harm yelled. He grabbed a child and herded his mother toward one of the huts.

Talia swung another little one up in her arms and ran alongside him.

The women screamed, gathered their children and ran for the relative safety of their homes.

Even before all of the women and children had cleared the road, trucks, SUVs and Jeeps careened into the village center.

Men carrying AK-47s leaped to the ground and began firing rounds.

More screaming filled the air.

The boy Harm had pulled out of the way ran into his mother's arms and they raced into the darkness, farther away from the roaring engines and flying bullets.

Harm's heart leaped into his throat when he couldn't find Talia. Then she appeared at his side, carrying a small child.

The kid was crying, tears streaming down her face.

"I don't know where her mother is." Talia held the child clutched to her breast, breathing hard from her mad dash. "They came so fast, I had to get her out of the way or she'd have been run over."

"You did the right thing." Harm pulled them behind one of the stick-and-mud huts on the far edge of the village. "Wait here. I want to find out what's going on."

More sounds of gunfire ripped through the air.

Talia ducked lower, shielding the child's body with her own. She reached out and touched his arm. "Don't go. They might shoot anyone standing."

"I'll stay in the shadows. They won't see me."

"Maybe not, but they don't seem too concerned about where they're shooting. They might hit you with a random shot."

"Trust me. I've done this before." He stared down at her. "As for you, stay in the shadows. I'll be right back."

She huddled with the child, both looking small and vulnerable.

Harm couldn't leave them for long. But he had to know if others needed help getting away from the attack. The women were defenseless, unarmed and burdened with the care of their children.

Harm pulled his pistol from the holster strapped to his calf and moved from shadow to shadow, working his way back toward the village center.

A toddler staggered between the buildings, crying hysterically.

Harm made his way toward the child and would have scooped him up, but a woman ran out of the darkness, snatched the baby up into her arms and turned to run back into the shadows, when a man wielding a rifle stepped in front of her and shouted, pointing his gun at the woman.

Harm didn't hesitate—he charged the man with the rifle, coming at him from his left side. The man didn't see him until Harm hit him in the side like a linebacker. At the same time, Harm grabbed the rifle, shoving the barrel toward the ground.

The attacker pulled the trigger, a bullet spitting up dust at their feet as they both crashed to the ground.

The man struggled beneath Harm's weight, but he couldn't wiggle free of Harm's hold.

Once the woman and her child got away, Harm knew he had to extricate himself. He didn't dare kill the man when he didn't know if he'd actually harmed anyone else. Every instinct told him to take the man out, but he wasn't on a mission. He wasn't authorized to use deadly force. For all he knew, the man could be one of the local rangers or some other authority. If he killed the man, he could set off an international incident involving the US Navy where they had no business fighting. Until he had a better grasp on the situation, he had to free his captive and let him go.

Harm silently counted to three, sprang to his feet, ripped the rifle out of the gunman's hands and flung it into tall grasses near the edge of the village.

The gunman staggered to his feet and ran toward the village center, yelling at the top of his voice.

"Time to leave," Harm muttered. He hurried back to where he'd left Talia.

She was there, but the child was gone.

"Oh, thank God." She flung herself into his arms.

He held her for only a second. "Where's the child?"

"Her mother found us and took her into the brush."

"We have to leave," Harm said. "Now."

"But how? The vehicle is at the end of the village. We have to get to it."

"Then we'll get there." He took her hand. "Stay with me and keep to the shadows." By freeing the gunman, he'd made his presence known. That he was at the Women Against Poaching rally would probably make it worse for the participants. Or he could be the bait to lure them away from the village. But if he was bait, that made Talia just as much of a target.

"It might be better if you hide in the brush and I come back later for you. They'll be after me."

"Why would they be after you?" Talia leaned into his body, her fingers holding tightly to his.

"I might have roughed up one of their own," he said and eased to the corner of a hut. "Any reason the truck might not start on the first try?"

"No. It's always turned over immediately. Why?"

"We'll need to get out of Dodge faster than the gunmen can shoot."

"That doesn't sound very promising."

"You're right. I'm going to stash you in the brush and come back for you after I lose these goons."

"You're not leaving me anywhere. We came to this dance together, we'll leave together. My mother always told me to leave with the one who brought me." She squeezed his hand. "I'm not letting go, so you might as well get used to it."

Harm liked that the woman had backbone, but he didn't like that they might be surrounded and not get out of the village on their own steam.

TALIA RAN TO keep up with Harm, afraid she'd slow him down and get them both killed. By the time they reached the other end of the village, she was breathing hard.

She'd parked her truck beside a hut, but they had to cross the road to get to it.

The men in the trucks and SUVs were still at the center of the village yelling and firing off rounds into the air.

As far as Talia could tell, they hadn't taken any hostages, or she'd have insisted on staying to see if there was anything she could do to help. The best thing they could do now was to lure the gunmen out of the village. If that meant setting themselves up as targets, at least that would redirect the violence away from the women and children who'd scattered into the brush to keep their families safe.

"Ready?" Harm asked.

She nodded and then realized he couldn't hear that. "Yes."

"On the count of three."

She bunched her muscles, ready to run.

Harm was silent for a second and then whispered, "Three."

He took off running, pulling her along with him.

They'd made it all the way across the road and had their hands on the truck door handles when a shout sounded. Gunfire sounded like so many tiny blasts, filling the night.

Harm sent Talia around to the other side of the truck, putting the bulk of the vehicle between her and the bullets.

He dived into the driver's seat and reached for the key.

The ignition was empty.

"Here." Talia shoved the key in and twisted it.

The engine fired up and roared to life.

Harm whipped the shift into gear and kicked up gravel and dust behind them as he spun away from the hut and onto the road. "Stay down!" he yelled.

Talia ducked low in her seat as bullets pinged against the metal truck body. Her heart raced and her hands shook as she remained bent double in the passenger seat, worrying about Harm, who had to sit up high enough to see over the dashboard.

A round pierced the back seats and flew all the way through the middle of the truck to hit the front windshield, leaving a jagged marble-size hole.

Talia's breath lodged in her throat and she gulped back the fear threatening to overwhelm her. She couldn't lose it now. She wasn't in as much danger as Harm. The least she could do was not panic and make his job even harder.

But it was hard not to panic. Those maniacs were still shooting at them.

The truck picked up speed, putting distance between them and the attackers.

Harm didn't say a word. His jaw was set in hard lines and his eyes shifted between the road ahead and the side mirrors. He pushed the accelerator all the way to the floor, rocketing them away from the village.

Talia dared to glance up into her side mirror. It had been hit by a stray bullet and the glass was cracked, but she could still see that the vehicles that had entered the village were now leaving—following them!

Go faster, she urged Harm silently. *Much faster!*

The road twisted and turned through acacia trees and brush and around termite mounds. Soon they'd be hitting the wide-open spaces of the savanna, where they'd be easy to shoot at and nothing would stand in the way.

They still had a long way to go to reach the resort, and when they did, the rest of the team would have no warning to let them know to be prepared to stand and defend. Besides, this attack wasn't the SEALs' responsibility. Unfortunately, Talia didn't even have any armed guards left to protect the resort. Perhaps she had overestimated her ability to run All Things Wild without a man to lean on. Nothing like this had ever happened when Michael was alive. Why was it happening now?

The engine coughed and sputtered.

"What's that?" she asked.

"We're losing oil pressure. One of those bullets probably hit the oil pan."

"Without oil, the engine will burn up." As the words left her mouth, Talia could smell the acrid scent of something burning. "Seriously? Why can't we limp along fast enough to reach the resort? At least there, we have more weapons. We stand a chance of defending ourselves."

"Sorry, darlin', but that's not going to be one of our choices."

"Figures." She sat up and stared into the side mirror. "We might not have more than a minute to come up with a plan."

"I'm ditching the truck. We can hide in the brush."

"That will be the first place they look."

"They will be looking for us to hide next to or ahead of the truck. We're going to backtrack in the direction of the village. Right now, I need to ditch the truck and hope they don't find it. Hold on." He shut off the headlights and shifted into Low to slow the vehicle without pressing the brakes, which would shine the brake lights, giving away their position.

For a few hundred more yards, he let the vehicle

decelerate until it was going slowly enough to roll off the road without flipping and killing them.

Talia gripped the armrest on the door as they bumped off the dirt road into the tall grass. She glanced behind them. Anyone with half a brain would see the trail they left in the grasses the truck mowed over. Hiding the vehicle would be impossible. They had to get out and hide themselves.

Once the truck came almost to a complete stop, Harm glanced over at her. "Jump."

Talia shoved open her door and threw herself out of the rolling vehicle. She hit the ground on her side, rolled and came up on her feet, searching for Harm.

The truck continued to roll forward. Once it had passed, the light from the stars overhead shined down on Harm's head.

Talia breathed a sigh and stepped into his arms.

He held her for a brief moment and then took her hand. "We have to get as far away from this truck as we can before they find it."

She nodded and fell in step with Harm as he jogged through the tall grass back toward the village. They ran twenty yards from the road but parallel to its path, hunkering below the tips of the tall grasses.

Harm raised his head over the tops of the grass fronds every so often to gauge where they were in comparison to the dirt road and the oncoming head-lights.

Within two minutes of them abandoning the

truck, the convoy of five vehicles roared past. Talia's heart leaped to her throat.

Harm grabbed her arm and pulled her down to her haunches until the last vehicle had gone by.

Harm slowly straightened, peering after the vehicles. "They blasted past, missing the point where we drove the truck off into the grass."

Talia breathed a sigh of relief.

"No, wait. One of them is backing up." He bent over and parted the fronds slightly. "Make that two... no, all of them have come about."

Talia tugged on his pant leg. "We should go."

Harm helped her to a crouching position and led the way, hurrying away from the truck and the gang of gunmen. They hadn't gone far when the rapid report of gunfire made them drop down to hug the earth.

Harm covered Talia's body with his own, pressing her harder into the dirt.

She could barely breathe, he was so heavy on her. If they were firing at them, Harm's body would take the bullets. "Don't." Talia squirmed beneath him, her voice lost in the noise of the barrage of bullets being expended.

Harm shifted and lifted his body off hers, then rose to check out what was going on.

"Are you crazy?" Talia whispered. "You'll get killed."

"They aren't shooting at us. I'm sorry to say this, but they're killing your truck."

"My truck?" Talia sat up and parted the grass.

From what little she could see, the men stood in a semicircle around what she assumed was her truck—she couldn't see it for the tall grass and the gun-toting men. But they were firing every round of ammunition they owned. One man even expelled his magazine and loaded another to shoot all the bullets in that one as well.

"My truck," Talia moaned. "Do you know how hard it is to get a good one for a reasonable price?" She sat back on the ground, feeling tears welling in her eyes. "Can't catch a stinkin' break."

"They're turning around. Get down." Once again, Harm threw his body over hers as bullets peppered the grass and brush in a 360-degree radius around the doomed truck.

When the gunfire ceased, Harm remained on top of her, facing the direction of the gang. "They're spreading out, trampling the grass. Time to move again," he said.

On hands and knees, they crawled away from the men searching for them.

When they'd gone a couple hundred yards, Harm rose to a crouch, clasped Talia's hand in his and led her farther away at a faster pace.

Talia glanced back to see headlights coming their direction. "They're on their way back toward the village."

"Hopefully just to pass through this time. They made their point the first time they came."

"What if the villagers have returned to their huts? We need to get there and warn them."

"Without a vehicle," Harm said, "we won't make it in time. And my bet is the truck is totaled."

"Then we shouldn't try to go back to the village. We might as well head home." Talia turned back and trudged toward the All Things Wild Resort, her feet already tired and her spirit tattered. When they came abreast of the truck, she fought back the tears, telling herself it was just an inanimate object, not a person. She had no reason to be as upset as she was.

Harm slipped an arm around her waist and pulled her against him. "I'm sorry about your truck," he said in a low, resonant tone that warmed the cool night air. She felt something warm against her hair and realized he'd pressed his lips to her head. *Why stop there?* she wanted to say. Instead, she tipped her head up to him and stared into his eyes, shining in the starlight.

He cupped her cheeks in his palms and brushed a tear away with the pad of his thumb.

Talia hadn't even realized the tears had fallen until Harm swiped one away.

"You can replace a vehicle," he said. "Don't let it get you down." He kissed her forehead.

Again, Talia wanted more. She lifted her chin higher. If he tried to kiss her forehead again, he'd have to settle for her lips.

For a long moment, he stared down into her eyes and then his gaze shifted lower.

Her breath caught and held in her throat. This was the moment of reckoning. If he didn't kiss her, she'd already decided to make the move herself. Her curiosity and the raging fire inside would not let him walk away again.

"I have no right to do this," he whispered. "You've already lost so much."

Beyond patience, Talia rose up on her toes, hooked the back of Harm's neck and pulled him down to meet her lips in a kiss that could only be described as a coming together of two very hungry people.

It started out desperate and raw, and several long, mindless minutes later, it ended just as it began— raw and edgy.

Chapter Eight

Talia pressed the back of her hand to her throbbing lips, her eyes wide, her breath coming in shallow gasps. "What the heck just happened?"

"I don't know. You tell me," Harm said.

Talia squeaked, her cheeks burning with embarrassment. "Did I ask that out loud?"

Harm chuckled. "You did."

She turned her hand over and touched her lips. "I've wanted to do that for too long."

"And now that you have?" He slipped his hands around her waist and pulled her hips against his.

She could feel the hard evidence of his desire dig into her belly and an answering response burn all the way to her core. "I want to do it again."

He bent his head, his mouth hovering over hers. "What are you waiting for?"

She shook her head, her desire pushing the guilt to the back of her mind. Again, she rose up on her toes, only this time she didn't have as far to go. Harm met her halfway there, his lips claiming hers in a kiss so hot, it left Talia burning for more.

His tongue traced the seam of her lips until she opened to let him in. He pushed past her teeth and caressed her tongue in a long, sensual sweep.

Talia melted into him, her knees weak, her heart racing. If Harm hadn't been holding her around her waist, she might have slipped to the ground in a boneless heap. Standing in the middle of a field, with the potential of bad guys returning to finish them off, Talia didn't care and she didn't want the kiss to end.

Too soon, the need to breathe superseded her desire. Talia tipped back her head and dragged in a shaky breath. "What are you doing to me?"

He chuckled, the low resonance of the sound reverberating in her chest where it touched his. "I should ask you the same question."

She laid her cheek against his shirt and listened to the pounding of his heartbeat. He was as affected by the kiss as she had been. For some reason, that made her strangely happy.

Talia drew in another deep breath and let it out before she stepped back far enough that he was forced to relinquish his hold. Immediately, she wished his hands were back around her waist, dipping low on her backside. How she wanted to be much closer. But they were a long way from the resort. By the time they walked there, it would be the wee hours of the morning. Another day would be upon her and, with it, all the chores and duties of a business owner with only the chef to help. The happiness of moments before was weighed down by the extent of her responsibilities.

"Are you ready for a stroll in the starlight?" Harm held out his arm.

Talia smiled and took it. "It's too bad we can't call a cab." As soon as she spoke the words, she remembered. "Wait. I might have a solution. If it wasn't destroyed." She strode to the bullet-ridden truck and dug in the console between the front seats. At the bottom of the storage compartment was the satellite phone she'd placed there earlier that day when they'd gone out on safari.

"Can you believe it?" She held it up triumphantly. "It doesn't have a single scratch."

Harm laughed. "I could kiss you."

"What are you waiting for?" she said, parroting his words of a moment before.

He pulled her into his arms and dropped a quick kiss on her lips. Then he set her at arm's length. "Make that call."

She hit the numbers that would connect her with the resort. Jamba answered on the fourth ring. "All Things Wild Resort."

"Jamba. What are you still doing at the resort? I thought you'd have gone home by now."

"I stayed to prep for the meals tomorrow. I was about to step out the door when the phone rang. What's wrong, Mrs. Talia?"

Talia told him what had occurred in the village

and then on the road home, and how they were stuck without transportation back to the resort. "Could you bring the spare truck to pick us up?"

"I'll try. I was going to take it home, if it would start."

"Are we still having trouble with the starter?"

"Yes, ma'am. If I can't get it going, I'll call someone to come get you two."

Talia told him approximately where they could be found and ended the call. The silence of the night surrounded her again. "Jamba will make sure someone comes to collect us."

"In the meantime, we might as well get comfortable." Harm glanced around. Shell casings littered the ground around the truck, like so much shiny confetti that could easily twist an ankle.

"It might be a good idea to stay away from the truck in case the gunmen return to look for us," he suggested.

"Agreed. But we can't go too far, since this is where I told Jamba to come."

They settled in the grass the length of a football field away from the destroyed truck, but closer to the road. From where they were, they could see headlights coming long before the drivers or occupants could see them.

Harm sat on the ground beside Talia and slid an arm around her. "You can lean against me and sleep, if you'd like."

"After all that's happened today, I don't think I'll

ever sleep again." Nevertheless, she leaned into his hard body. "I'm glad you insisted on coming with me tonight." Despite the chaos of the evening, a yawn overtook her and she closed her eyes. "I don't know if I would have tried to make a run for it in the truck. Because of your decision to leave, I'm sure the village women had a better chance of escaping once we led the gunmen out of the village."

"I'm glad I came, too. The thought of you dealing with what happened by yourself would have made me sick with worry."

She laughed. "You wouldn't have known it was happening."

"Which would make me even more worried, imagining all the possibilities." He sighed. "Not that I would have come up with any imaginary scenarios close to the reality of what went down tonight."

"What a disaster. The women of the village will never want to stand up to anyone again. Not when there are gunmen shooting at them and their children."

"We need to come back during the daylight and ask questions. I want to talk with the witch doctor and the men of the village. They seemed suspiciously absent tonight."

"Hopefully, the gunmen were only there to scare the women into submission."

"Shooting up your truck and then firing into the field went beyond scare tactics."

Talia nodded. She prayed they hadn't returned to

the village to do more damage. Perhaps when Jamba arrived with the spare truck, she'd head back to the village and make certain the women and children were all right.

HARM SAT IN the starlight, holding Talia. Not long afterward, he could feel her relax against him, so much so that she had to be asleep.

He studied her slight frame in the meager light, wishing he could do more to protect the woman. She was brave beyond measure, but he feared she was careless about her own life.

Less than an hour after Talia placed the call to the resort, headlights appeared, coming from the direction they'd been heading when their truck had given out.

Though he was expecting the truck from All Things Wild, Harm still wasn't taking any chances. He squeezed Talia's shoulder and whispered in her ear, "We need to move."

She startled awake, her gaze shooting to his. "What? What's happened?"

He laughed. "You fell asleep. But someone's coming."

She glanced toward the oncoming orbs and rubbed her eyes. "That will be Jamba."

"I'm not taking any chances. When I know for sure, I'll let him see me. Until then, I want you to stay here and lie low." He pushed to his feet.

Her hand caught his. "You're not staying with me?"

"I'm going to get closer to the truck. He will stop there first, because that's where he expects to find us."

"I'd rather stay with you."

Harm shook his head. "It's too dangerous."

She tilted her head to the side and narrowed her eyes. "I could be attacked by lions, you know."

Harm thought for a moment and then sighed. "You're damned if you do and damned if you don't." He jerked his head to the side. "Come on."

Talia leaped to her feet and hurried after him.

Together, they hunkered below the tall grass fronds and ran toward the pickup. The headlights were moving fast, closing in on them.

By the time the vehicle came to a halt near the road where the grass had been mowed down by the truck, Harm and Talia were safely concealed in the thick grass, several feet away from the damaged truck.

Jamba dropped down out of the driver's seat at the same time as the entire SEAL team leaped to the ground.

"Harm! Talia!" Big Jake called out.

Harm chuckled and straightened. "Over here."

Talia stood beside him, grinning. "You really do have each other's backs, don't you?"

"Damn right, we do." Harm strode out of the grass onto the road where the SEALs stood, each holding a weapon.

"You look like you're on a mission," Harm said.

"We are," Diesel responded. "A mission to rescue one of our own."

"You're a little late."

"The story of our lives." T-Mac circled the truck. "It appears we missed all the fun."

"Damn, Harm, you could've saved some for us," Buck said.

"Would've if I could've." Harm pulled Talia close. "But we were too busy trying to survive."

"Then I suppose we'll cut you some slack this time." Pitbull whistled. "They did a number on Talia's truck."

"You weren't in it at the time, were you?" Big Jake looked away from the truck to study Harm and Talia.

"No, thank goodness," Talia said.

"The main thing is, you came." Harm held out his hand to Big Jake. "Thanks."

Big Jake took his hand and pulled him into a hug. "Wouldn't have let Jamba go on a mission by himself." He released Harm and grinned at the chef. "We're thinking of making him an honorary SEAL. He drove like a bat out of hell to get here as fast as he could."

"I would have been here sooner if the starter hadn't given me troubles," Jamba said. "That's why I haven't turned off the engine."

Talia shook her head. "I guess that's at the top of my to-do list."

"Between Marly and T-Mac, they ought to be able to help you," Pitbull said.

"I ordered a spare starter. It should be in any day

now." Talia yawned. "I'm sorry. I guess I'm more exhausted than I thought." She leaned into Harm.

He tightened his hold on her, loving the way she felt pressed against his body.

Talia yawned again. "And I'm sorry we disturbed your evening to come rescue us."

"No worries," Big Jake said. "There weren't enough womenfolk to go around on the dance floor, and some of the guys weren't sharing. We needed a little excitement."

"Speak for yourself," Buck said. "I had excitement in my arms and will again, when we get back to the resort."

"Speaking of which," Harm said, "let's get back. I'm sure Talia has an early morning planned."

"If it has to be because of us, don't worry. We can fend for ourselves," Big Jake assured her. "We've been doing it for years."

"Yeah. I can make toast," Pitbull said. "And we've all been trained to make our own beds."

Buck puffed out his chest. "I can bounce a quarter off my sheets when I put my mind to doing it right."

Talia laughed. "I might take you up on that. But I do need to get back, and you all need a good night's sleep. We're supposed to go out on safari again in that truck tomorrow."

"If it's all the same to you, we could use some downtime," T-Mac said. "We have yet to use the pool, and my tan is woefully pale."

"I'm up for a swim and a long nap in the sun," Pitbull agreed.

Big Jake nodded. "We can save the safari thing for when we're sure the truck won't leave us stranded somewhere in the middle of a herd of angry cape buffalo."

Harm smiled at his team. He couldn't have asked for a better group of men to fight, live and play at his side. He loved being a part of this brotherhood.

He took Talia's hand in his and squeezed it gently. "Then it's settled. No safari tomorrow. That frees up the truck—once it's fixed—for me to go into the village in daylight and ask a few questions."

Talia grinned. "Thanks." She let him help her up into the passenger seat next to Jamba.

"What about you, Jamba?" she asked. "You need a way to get home tonight."

"I can stay at the resort. As late as it is, it doesn't make sense for me to drive home, turn around and drive back just a few hours later."

"Jamba, you really are a gentleman," Talia said.

"An honorary SEAL." The chef lifted his chin and waited while the others climbed aboard.

Talia laughed, the sound filling Harm's heart with hope.

She was an amazing woman. To have lived through what had happened tonight and still be able to laugh showed what stern stuff she was made of. The more he saw of her, the more Harm liked. If he wasn't careful, he could fall in love with the woman.

On the trip back to the resort, Harm kept a vigilant watch over the road ahead, on alert in case the men who'd attacked them earlier had circled around to head them off. By the time they arrived in the re-sort compound, Harm was wound tighter than an old-fashioned top. He was out of the truck before it came to a complete stop.

Talia pushed open her door. Before she could drop down, Harm caught her around the waist and lowered her to the ground.

She remained in his grip, her body pressed against his for a long moment.

"Anyone up for a beer?" T-Mac asked.

Talia pulled away and pushed her hair back from her face in a nervous gesture.

"Not me," Pitbull said. "I'm hitting the sack."

"Me, too," Buck said.

"That's right, rub it in." T-Mac shook his head. "You have women. We don't." He turned to Big Jake. "Beer, big guy?"

"Not me. All the excitement today wore me out."

"Seriously? Dude, you're getting old." T-Mac slung an arm over Diesel's shoulders. "Looks like it's just the two of us. Care to play a friendly game of pool? I'll spot you two balls."

"Keep your balls, I'm calling it a night," Diesel said. "I gotta rest up for the sunbathing I'm going to do tomorrow."

Harm chuckled. T-Mac turned to him, his brows raised.

Harm shook his head. "I'm looking for a shower and pillow." He wasn't really sleepy, but he wanted to keep pace with Talia. If she was headed up to her room, he was, too.

"Talia?" T-Mac asked, his tone that of a man who already knew the answer.

"Sorry. I'm dirty and sleepy. Maybe tomorrow night, when I haven't been used for target practice."

T-Mac's shoulders slumped. "Then I'll call it a night."

"If you ask me nicely, I'll check your cabin before you go in," Diesel said.

"Diesel, sweet cheeks, will you snake-proof my cabin for me?" T-Mac asked in a falsetto that had the other guys laughing out loud.

Diesel rolled his eyes. "Yes, but keep the girl talk to a minimum."

"Aye, aye, sailor." T-Mac popped a salute and then ruined it with a wink. "Night, all." He left the group with Diesel bringing up the rear.

Jamba claimed one of the empty cabins for the night. Buck and Pitbull hurried off to their cabins, where their women waited for them.

Big Jake was already halfway up the stairs when Harm and Talia entered the lodge.

Which left Harm and Talia alone on the ground floor.

Talia glanced toward the kitchen. "I should check to see that everything is in order for breakfast in the morning."

Harm gripped her arms. "Give Jamba a little credit. That man runs a tight kitchen."

She sighed and rested her hands on his chest. "You're right. Besides, I'm too tired to care right now."

He liked how warm her fingers were through his shirt. "Then go to bed," he said, his voice husky.

She stared at her hands where they rested, as if avoiding his gaze. "It's hard to walk away without knowing exactly what I'll have to deal with in the morning."

"I'm sure you can handle anything. But you'd do it even better on a decent night's sleep." He released one arm to brush a strand of her hair back from her forehead.

She laughed, the sound breathy and maybe a little shaky. "Okay, okay, you don't have to twist my arm. I'll shower and then go straight to bed."

Still, Harm couldn't bring himself to let go. He could still feel the panic that had overtaken him when he couldn't find her in the village. "I'm sorry about what happened in the village tonight."

"It's not your fault," she said. "I'm just glad you were there to help." She finally glanced up, meeting his gaze.

He felt as if he were teetering on the edge of a precipice, on the verge of falling into the deep, blue depths of her eyes. "About that kiss," he said without thinking.

"You don't have to apologize," she hurried to say.

"I wasn't going to." Harm chuckled. "What would you say if—" he lowered his head until his lips hovered a breath away from hers "—I asked if I could kiss you again?"

"I might regret it later, but I'd probably say, what are you waiting for?" She raised up on her toes, wrapped her arms around his neck and pressed her lips to his.

The moment her mouth touched his, a storm of desire ripped through his body, spreading fire along every nerve ending, pooling low in his groin. He wanted her in the most primal way.

Harm buried his fingers in her thick, luxurious hair, dragging her head backward, exposing her neck. He left her mouth to trail kisses down the length of her throat to the base, where her pulse beat like a snare drum in a marching band.

Footsteps on the stairs behind him finally pierced the haze of longing and made Harm lift his head.

Talia stepped back and pressed her palms to her cheeks.

Big Jake stopped halfway down the stairs, his lips twsiting. "I seem to be making this a habit. I didn't know you two were still down here." He started to turn around.

Talia hurried toward him. "No, don't go. It's okay. We were just…" She glanced toward Harm.

"Saying good-night," Harm said. He grabbed her hand and led her up the stairs and past Big Jake.

"If you need anything in the kitchen, you can help yourself," Talia called out over her shoulder.

The rumbling sound of Big Jake's chuckle followed Harm and Talia all the way up the landing and to Harm's bedroom door.

Now that they were out of Big Jake's sight, Harm pulled Talia into his arms again.

She shook her head. "We shouldn't."

"Name one reason why we shouldn't," he challenged her.

She opened her mouth to speak, but nothing came out.

"I can give you at least a dozen reasons why we should." He kissed the tip of her nose. "Because you're beautiful. Because I can't seem to resist you. Because I like the way your nose wrinkles when you frown. Because your eyes turn a darker shade of blue just before you kiss me. Because we're not getting any younger. Because there's something happening I can't explain. And because you can't go through life second-guessing yourself. Sometimes you have to go with your gut." He pressed his forehead to hers.

"And what is your gut saying to you?" she asked.

"It's telling me to make love to you. Now. Before my brain engages and tells me otherwise." He lifted his head and brushed her forehead with his lips. "What's your gut telling you?" He closed his eyes and wished for the answer his heart desired.

"It's telling me to go for it, but my mind is telling me to get a shower and go to bed. Alone."

"We could take this one step at a time." He swept

his knuckles down her cheek and the length of her neck, stopping to rest on her beating pulse.

She leaned back her head, giving him better access. "What do you mean?"

"You need a shower." He poked his thumb to his chest. "I need a shower. We could conserve water and take one together."

Her lips curled upward. "You make a good argument. And we always need to conserve water on the savanna."

"Then what are we waiting for?"

She pulled her bottom lip between her teeth. "We're waiting for my gut to overrule my head."

Harm drew in a long, slow breath and let it out a little at a time. "As much as I want to throw you over my shoulder and march with you into the shower...if you're not ready, you're not ready. And I won't take advantage of you."

He kissed the tip of her nose and leaned away from her.

"Wait." She touched a hand to his chest. "I didn't say I wasn't ready."

"I can read your body language. You're hesitating. I don't want to be the focus of your regrets. Whatever we have between us must be based on our own attraction, the merit of the two of us...together."

She stared up into his eyes for a long moment. Then she took his hand. "One more reason to fall into this relationship is because you're willing to wait when I can't find the words to express how I feel. Because when you kiss me, I can't think of anything else besides getting completely naked with you and making love until the dawn rises on the eastern horizon."

Before she could say another word, he was leading her into his room and the connecting bathroom. Once there, he slipped her shirt up over her head and tossed it over the towel bar. He ripped his own shirt over his head and let it fall to the floor.

Her fingers wrapped around the button on his jeans. She gripped the zipper and eased it downward until his staff sprang free of the tight confines. Talia wrapped her hand around his erection and squeezed gently.

Harm moaned and leaned his head back, savoring the feel of her warm hands on his hardness. He didn't want her to stop. The only thing that could feel better was to be buried deep inside her.

He reached for the button on her jeans and slipped it loose, not wasting any time removing the remainder of her clothing. As soon as he'd stripped her, he shucked his own clothing and turned on the faucet in the tiled shower stall. He held out his hand to her. "It's up to you. Come or go. Leave or stay. I won't be mad, or think any less if you decide now isn't the right time."

"Seriously?" She laughed and placed her hand in

his. "I thought the time to back out was before we got naked."

Harm laughed with her. Not only was she beautiful, she had a sense of humor. Could the woman be any more perfect?

Chapter Nine

Harm smiled into her eyes, the rumble of his laughter a quiet echo in the room.

Talia loved that he could joke as they stood next to the shower in nothing but their birthday suits. He didn't make her feel awkward or insecure. Since she hadn't been out on a date or with another man since before she married her husband, the whole business of getting to know each other was fairly new to her.

"No kidding, Talia. I can still be swayed by a simple no. But mark my words," he said. "I won't give up easily. I go after what I want. And I want you."

Her gaze slipped from his eyes to his mouth. She didn't want to say it, but she couldn't help herself. "You haven't mentioned a word about love."

Harm shook his head. "That might take a little longer. You see, where you think you might not be ready, there's an equally big hesitation on my part. When my fiancée dumped me for another guy, I swore I wouldn't fall for that kind of relationship again. What I feel for you is purely physical."

Talia's chest tightened. She'd bet he was afraid of love and commitment. She spread her hand over his heart, her fingers warm against his skin. "Are you sure?" she whispered.

"Sweetheart, I know I want you. That's a one hundred percent certainty." He looked away. "Anything else, I can't say for sure. Can we leave it at that? I'm not asking you for commitment, nor am I promising the same. If that's a deal breaker, speak now."

With a sigh, Talia slid her hand up to circle around the back of his neck. "It's not a deal breaker. It's just that I've never been in a purely physical relationship." She leaned up on her toes and touched her lips to his in a feather-soft kiss. The caress was over almost before it began, yet she wanted more. "How do you guard your heart, to keep it from breaking?"

"You leave your heart out of it," he said in a harsh tone. "This is all about the needs of a man and a woman."

Someone really must have hurt the man to make him so cynical. Though she still had love in her heart for Michael, she couldn't deny her attraction to Harm. "Mmm. I have needs. But they aren't all physical." She pulled him down for another teasing kiss. Her breasts brushed against his chest, causing electricity to shoot straight to her core.

It must have hit him, too, because his shaft grew longer and harder. She'd bet he could drive nails with it. Her lips quirked at the image in her mind.

"Shouldn't we get under the water before it grows cold?" she prompted.

Harm sucked in a steadying breath and stepped under the spray, bringing Talia with him.

The water drenched them, running in rivulets over their shoulders.

Talia studied the paths the little tributaries took as gravity led them downward. Across the massive planes of his chest, down the rock-hard abs to where his shaft jutted out, strong and full.

Her breath caught and held in her throat. As if of their own accord, her hands rose and wrapped around Harm's thick erection.

He sucked in a sharp breath and surged up into her grip.

She loved how he responded to her touch. It gave her a sense of power. Slowly, she stroked him, sliding her fingers the length of him and back to the base.

He closed his eyes and tilted his head back, letting the warm water glide over his body and hers.

Then he poured shampoo into his hands and rubbed it into her hair.

Talia almost moaned at the wonderful feeling of someone massaging her scalp. She basked in the attention. Michael had never washed her hair for her. They'd been too busy running the resort to slow down long enough to think much about the other's desires.

Harm rinsed the bubbles free and applied conditioner.

Almost giddy with delight, Talia couldn't help but

wonder what man remembered that long hair needed conditioner in order to ease out the tangles?

Once Harm finished washing her hair, he grabbed the bar of soap, worked up a lather and slid his hands along her neck, over her collarbone and across the swells of her breasts.

She pushed into his palms, urging him to take more.

He did, lightly pinching the tips of her nipples between his thumbs and forefingers.

Her body answered with a resounding tug low in her belly, her core tightening with every move. Soon, she realized that foreplay took far too long. She wanted him. Now. Having gone more than a year since she'd been sexually satisfied, she didn't have the strength to wait any longer.

She resumed her grip on his erection, tightened her hand and moved faster, until she was pumping along like a piston engine.

"Can't do this." Harm grabbed her wrist and lifted her hand free of his shaft. He spun her around and doused her beneath the water, rinsing all the suds from her body.

She soaped him and traded places. Once they were both clean and suds-free, Harm turned off the water and wrapped Talia in a towel. He lifted her out of the shower and set her on the bath mat, then stepped out to stand beside her.

They dried each other off, laughing when arms and legs got in the way. Still damp in some places, they came together in a soul-defining kiss Talia never wanted to end.

But it did, with better things to come.

Harm scooped her up in his arms, carried her into the bedroom and laid her on the bed.

She scooted back and made room for him, her heart pounding, her nerves stretched. This was the moment of reckoning. A year was a long time to go between lovemaking. What if she'd forgotten how to please a man? What if the only man who could please her was Michael?

Her breathing grew strangled, and her body stiffened.

"Hey." Harm pressed a kiss to her forehead. "We don't have to take it any further. You can back out now, if it will make you feel better."

"No, that's not it. I'm just nervous." She laughed shakily. "I feel like this is my first time, all over again."

"And it is…with me." He nibbled her earlobe and trailed a line of kisses along her jaw until he reached her lips, where he paused. "Are you feeling it yet?"

"Uh, no?" She stared up at him. "Maybe this will help." She curled her fingers around the back of his neck and closed the short distance between their mouths.

Yes. This was where she'd wanted to be.

He leaned over her, his chest pressing against hers, warming her in the cool of the air-conditioned room. Where his body touched hers, she could feel the fire building, burning a path to her center. "Better," she said against his lips.

He left her mouth to press kisses down the side of her neck to the base, where her pulse pounded against her skin.

Harm's hands led the way across her breasts, cupping each orb as if weighing it in his palm. Then he rolled her nipple between his fingers. He followed quickly with his mouth, taking the nipple between his teeth, nipping gently and then flicking it with the tip of his tongue.

Talia's back arched, her breasts rising up, urging him to take more.

He sucked the tip into his mouth and more, pulling hard and then letting go with a popping sound. While he treated the other breast to the same teasing, his fingers led the way again, sliding down her torso, skimming across her ribs, dipping into her belly button and coming to a stop over the mound of hair covering her sex.

Talia sucked in a breath and held it. Would he stop there? Oh, she hoped he didn't. Already her channel was slick and ready. He could take her now and she'd welcome him.

His mouth left her breast and followed his fingers' path down her body.

Her body on fire, Talia writhed beneath him. "Please," she moaned.

He chuckled. "Please what?"

"Enough with the appetizers. I want the whole enchilada."

Harm laughed out loud. "Way to kill the mood by talking about food."

"I'm sorry. I told you I was rusty." She still couldn't breathe, her body poised for his next move. And if he didn't make it soon, she might have to do it for him.

The SEAL parted her folds and blew a warm stream of air onto that heated strip of flesh.

Her body trembled, on the verge of something monumental. She raised her knees and let her legs fall open, willing him to come to her.

One big, callused finger dipped inside.

Talia almost cried out her relief that finally they were getting somewhere.

Then his tongue flicked her in just the right spot.

She dug her heels into the mattress and raised her hips. "There, oh yes. There," she called out.

He chuckled and flicked her again, then settled in to lick, stroke and tease her into a frenzy, all the while pumping his finger into her damp channel. He added another finger, then another, stretching her, hopefully for when he came inside her.

Which couldn't be soon enough.

Talia couldn't get air into or out of her lungs, but she didn't care. If she died then, she'd be completely satisfied.

Then he hit the magical sweet spot and sent her flying to the moon.

Talia grabbed the hair on his head and cried out, "Harm! Oh, yes! Oh, yes! Oh, yes!" Her body shook with her release, the spasms shooting through her in waves until she finally sank back to earth and the mattress. But she wasn't done yet. Nothing would be complete without Harm filling what had been empty for far too long.

Instead of slipping into her, the man rolled off the bed and stood.

"Holy hell, you can't leave now," she cried.

"We're in my room." He grinned and smoothed his hand over her fevered brow. "We need protection, and my wallet is on the dresser."

"Don't just stand there…get it," she commanded, her body already cooling in his absence.

Within seconds, Harm was back in the bed with a foil packet. He ripped it open and would have applied it himself. But Talia, already impatient beyond control, grabbed the condom from him and rolled it over his erection.

Harm nudged her knees apart and positioned himself between her legs. "You can still say no."

"No. I. Can't," she said in short, clipped tones. "I want you, Harmon Payne. If I have regrets in the morning, I'll deal with them then. For now, all I need is you. Inside me. Now."

He pressed his shaft to her entrance and eased into her.

Talia dragged air into her starving lungs and let it out slowly, letting her body adjust to his girth and the feeling of being full in the best possible way she could imagine.

Harm eased back out. Before he could slip free, she pulled him back.

He set a steady pace, increasing the speed and force with every thrust until he pounded in and out of her.

When she thought it couldn't get better, he thrust one last time and buried himself inside her, so deep she couldn't fathom where she ended and he began. It all felt so good and so...right.

When his shaft stopped throbbing and his body relaxed, Harm sank down onto her and rolled them both to their sides.

Talia inhaled a shaky breath. "Wow."

"I agree. Wow."

"It really is like riding a bicycle."

Harm's bark of laughter filled the room. "What?"

"You never forget. You just get back on and it all comes back. Only it's better than memories. It's real and visceral." She cupped his cheek and smiled. "Thank you."

He shook his head, his lips twitching at the corners. "That has to be the first time anyone has ever compared having sex with me to riding a bicycle."

Laughter bubbled up inside her. For the first time in a year, she felt young and alive again. "I'm sorry if it took the wind out of your sails, but you made me feel alive again. And if we never see each other again, I have you to thank for that."

HARM PULLED TALIA into the curve of his arm, where she rested her head on his shoulder and her cheek against his chest. She fit him perfectly. Not too tall, but small enough that she made him feel like he should protect her.

"Why do you think we'll never see each other again?"

She traced her finger around his nipple. "When would we have the opportunity? You have your job as a SEAL. I have the resort. I can't leave it to run by itself. Especially now that my staff has been scared off."

"But you could. Once we figure out why someone is putting the screws to you."

She shook her head. "In the eight years we've owned the resort, we haven't had a real vacation. We got away for a couple of weekends, but that was it. When you're a small-business owner, you live, eat and breathe the work."

Harm shook his head. "I can't imagine you being shackled to the resort for the rest of your life when there are so many more places to see and visit."

"But I'm not shackled. I can come and go as I please."

"If you have staff to do the work."

She sighed. "There's always some drama. This too will blow over. This has been my home for so long. I can't imagine leaving. I have nowhere else to go."

Harm's gut twisted. "I'm sorry. I know how hard

it is to lose loved ones. My father was killed by a drunk driver while I was in BUD/S."

Talia touched his cheek. "That's awful."

"I think the loss was what made me sick, but my mother insisted I stay and gut it out. She wouldn't let me quit, any more than I wanted to quit."

"She was right. You wouldn't be the man you are today if you quit. Your father would have been so proud of you."

Harm nodded. His father had grinned from ear to ear when Harm had told him he was going to BUD/S training. As a former marine, he knew what it took to make it through that training. Even to be selected for it, each candidate had to meet the highest standards.

"What about your in-laws?" Harm asked. "Where are they?"

"Michael was ten years older than I am. His parents died before we met."

"Siblings?"

She shook her head. "We were both only children."

"What about children?"

"None."

"Never wanted them?" Harm asked.

Talia gave him a sad smile. "Never got around to it. We were always so busy with running the resort, photography and safaris, there was never time to slow down and raise a child."

"You would make a good mother."

Talia laughed. "Why do you say that?"

"You have a big heart. I saw you with Eriku. You want so much for her. You gave her a job, taught her there was a world bigger than just her village. You have a lot to give to children."

"But to be a parent, you have to have the time to be with the children, to nurture and teach them what's important in life."

"Sometimes all it takes is showing them by example. Both my parents worked, but when they were with me, they loved me wholeheartedly. I learned so much from them by watching how they handled people, work and life."

"I always wanted to have children, but there never seemed to be the right time."

"I learned from other members of the SEAL brotherhood that you can't *plan* children. They just happen, and you adjust your life around them."

"Yeah, well, I'm sure that's what other people do. My husband is gone. I'm alone now and I'm getting too old to have children."

Harm had never thought to ask how old Talia was. She seemed so young and vibrant. "At the risk of being rude, just how old are you?"

"I'll be thirty-three next February."

Harm laughed. "Thirty-three? And you're too old to have children?"

Talia's eyes narrowed. "Most of the people I went to high school and college with have children almost in their teens."

"And I know more people who are waiting until they're in their forties to have children." Harm brushed a strand of her hair back behind her ear. "Trust me, you're not too old."

"I'm sure I'm older than you," she said. "I'm probably robbing the cradle. A cougar stalking a man child."

Harm frowned. "You're only two years older than I am."

"In dog years, that's fourteen years."

"Since when are you a dog?" He pressed his lips to hers. "You must be beyond exhaustion, because you're babbling and not making any sense."

"I make a lot of sense. I'm too old for you and I'm too old to have children, and I own a resort that needs me. My staff need the jobs the resort provides. I can't desert them. They depend on that money to support their families."

"If you don't make money, you can't afford to pay them."

"I know. I know." She closed her eyes. "Perhaps you're right. I need to sleep. Everything will work out in the morning."

Harm smoothed a hand over her hair. "That's right. Sleep. Knowing you, you'll be up at the crack of dawn, and that's only a few hours away."

Talia yawned, covering her mouth with her hand. "Harm?"

"Yes, sweetheart?"

"Will I see you again?" she whispered.

"I'm here all week," he replied.

"That's not really what I asked, but I guess you gave me your answer."

He would like to have said more, but the reality was, he'd leave at the end of the week, and he had no idea when he'd ever be back to Kenya, much less to the All Things Wild Resort.

The night seemed to get shorter, the possibilities drying up, only making him more depressed by the moment. The more he was with Talia, the more time he wanted to spend with her. A day wasn't enough. The week would be too short. A lifetime didn't seem enough, at that point.

Was it possible? Had he succumbed to love?

Chapter Ten

Too tired to keep her eyes open, and too comfortable and safe in Harm's embrace, Talia fell into a deep sleep, the likes of which she hadn't experienced since the death of her husband.

When she awoke, the sun shined in through the windows, bathing her in a warm, golden light.

She lay for a moment trying to get her bearings. The room didn't look right. It took several seconds for everything from the night before to rush back into her mind. She sat up straight in the bed and realized she was naked.

The door to the bedroom opened.

Talia yanked the sheet up over her bare breasts and stared wide-eyed at the man backing into the room, carrying a tray smelling of food and the rich aroma of coffee.

"I thought you might be hungry and in need of caffeine." Harm turned with a smile. The tray was laden with everything from scrambled eggs to pancakes and bacon, along with steaming mugs of coffee and two small glasses of orange juice.

"What time is it?" she asked.

"After seven o'clock."

"What?" She flung her legs over the side of the bed, hugging the sheet to her body. No matter how hard she pulled, she couldn't get the sheet to come untucked from the foot of the bed. If she wanted to stand, she'd have to abandon the sheet altogether and go naked.

Harm set the tray on the dresser. "Now, don't go getting your panties in a twist."

"I'm not wearing any panties," she hissed. "I think we left them in the bathroom."

With a chuckle, Harm crossed his arms over his chest. "Well, then I think you're in a pickle."

"Could you please hand me my clothing?" she asked. "I have a lot of work to do."

"As you can see, I'm quite busy serving a pretty lady her breakfast in bed. Otherwise I would comply." His lips twitched as if he was holding back a grin.

"Harmon Payne, you are no gentleman," she declared.

He nodded. "That's one thing we can agree on." Turning back to the tray, he asked, "Do you prefer sugar and cream in your coffee, or do you drink it black?"

Talia hefted a pillow from behind her and threw

it at the back of Harm's head. "You're so…so…" She struggled for the right expletive.

"Handsome? Thoughtful? Sexy?" He retrieved the pillow from the floor and tossed it back to her. "Now, how was it you liked your coffee?"

"Dressed in my own clothes."

"Maybe you'll take it black instead." He handed her the mug of coffee. "Be a good girl and sip it slowly. It's piping hot."

She glared at him but took the mug, the aroma too tantalizing to resist. As she reached for the mug, the sheet slipped, exposing one breast. Talia struggled to pull the sheet back in place, nearly spilling the coffee.

Harm tucked the sheet beneath her arm and winked. "You know, I've seen all of you."

"At night. All wet," she countered and took a sip of the coffee, careful not to burn her tongue. "And it's different."

"How so?" He tilted his head to the side, studying her. "You're the same person today as you were last night."

"Last night I was…" Again, words escaped her.

"Beautiful." Harm kissed her forehead. "Sexy." He kissed the tip of her nose. "Amazing." His lips found hers. Without breaking the lip-lock, he took the coffee mug from her hand, set it on the nightstand and kissed her thoroughly.

He tasted of coffee and bacon, making her tummy rumble. Talia couldn't fight what her body wanted.

She raised both arms, wrapped her hands behind his neck and pulled him down to her.

Harm lay on the bed beside her and dragged her into his arms, his hands gliding over her skin, warm, rough and igniting every nerve where he touched.

Talia forgot to be shy or embarrassed as her body awakened to Harm.

His kiss deepened, his tongue pushing past her teeth.

Talia opened to him, loving the taste, feel and strength of the man. She tangled her fingers in his hair in an effort to get even closer, but he was dressed for the day, not naked like her.

Harm's hand slipped down the small of her back to her bottom, where he smacked her lightly and pushed to a sitting position. "There's nothing I'd like better than to spend the day in bed, making love to you, but I'll bet that within the next twenty minutes or less, someone will come searching for you."

She sighed and pulled the sheet back up over her body. "I suppose you're right."

He stood, handed her the mug of coffee and pulled a long T-shirt out of his duffel bag. "You can wear this to get to your room and your own clothing."

Again, he took the mug and set it on the nightstand, then held the shirt over her head.

Talia raised her arms, letting the sheet drop around her waist. Part of her hoped it would be enough to entice the man to throw caution to the wind, strip naked and join her.

The shirt slipped over her head and arms and pooled around her hips. So much for dreaming lusty thoughts.

Harm brought the tray over and set it on the bed beside her. Together they ate the food Jamba had prepared, feeding each other like lovers.

Talia couldn't remember the last time someone had served her breakfast in bed. Probably her mother, bringing soup when she'd been a sick child.

She liked being treated like a cherished princess, if only for an hour. The man was chalking up a pile of points in his favor. Talia would have to guard her heart well or risk losing it to the SEAL.

Once they'd finished their breakfast in bed, Talia gathered her clothing and ran for her room down the hall. She had barely dressed when a knock on her door forced her to finish quickly.

"Mrs. Talia, Mrs. Talia, you have a visitor," Nahla's voice called out through the paneling.

Talia looked one last time at what her life had been and laid the photograph facedown on the nightstand. She crossed to open the door and found Nahla wringing her hands and staring over her shoulder at the staircase. When she realized Talia had opened the door, she gushed, "Mr. Krause from Pinnacle Ranch is in the great room. He wanted to talk with you. What do you want me to tell him?"

"I'm coming down. Did Jim say what he wanted?"

"No, ma'am. He just wanted to talk to you. He's down there now with the guests."

Talia's lips quirked. She could imagine Jim sitting among the navy SEALs. They'd overwhelm him with their size and the breadth of their shoulders.

Jim wasn't a small man, but he wasn't built like the SEALs. She wondered what they'd find to talk about.

With one last glance at her room, she hurried out the door and down the stairs to the great room where Jim Krause sat with the six navy SEALs, Angela and Marly.

Harm saw her first and stood. The rest of the men rose to their feet. Jim was last. He strode to her and extended a hand.

"Jim, it's good to see you. What's it been? Three months?" she asked.

"At least. We seem to be so caught up in our own businesses, it's hard to get out and pay our respects to the neighbors." His grip on her hand was cool and a little clammy, but firm almost to the point of hurting.

When he released her fingers, she moved her hand behind her back. "Would you like a cup of coffee?"

"No, thank you. I came by to see how you were. I understand there was some trouble in the village last night."

Talia nodded. "Apparently the village idiots don't like the idea of the women protesting the slaughter of protected animals."

Jim shook his head. "I don't know what it will take to get everyone on the same page for conservancy."

"The demand has to dry up or be jailed before

the poachers will quit poaching." She was stating the obvious, but Jim knew the stakes. "The poachers don't understand that when these animals are gone, there won't be any more to replace them. Not only will they become extinct, but the tourism industry will dry up and the locals will have no way to make enough money to feed their families."

Jim nodded. "The money is far too good to stop them now."

Talia knew this to be true. The danger to the animals was real, and not enough of the right people seemed to give a damn. "Yesterday, we came across a dead rhinoceros in the national preserve."

Jim's eyes narrowed. "Horns removed?"

Talia nodded, pressing her lips together in a tight line. "Such a waste of an animal, all for its horns and superstitious nonsense."

"When you can get thirty thousand dollars for a single horn, the money talks," Jim said.

"Yeah, but the poachers aren't getting that much. The middlemen are." Talia wrapped her arms around her midsection, aware Harm was standing close to her. His mere presence made her feel somehow protected.

"Still, the poachers are getting more for the horns than they can make in a year working at one of our resorts or ranches," Jim pointed out. He looked at her closer. "But how are you since Michael passed? I'm surprised you haven't sold this place and moved back to the States where it's much safer. Let me know when you're ready to sell. I'd be interested in taking the place off your hands."

"Thanks, Jim, but I haven't made that decision yet, and I'm not sure I will." In her peripheral vision, she could see Harm. She'd shared a heated moment with the man, but was it enough to leave behind her hopes and dreams for All Things Wild?

"Michael loved this place, but without him, you're exposed. Though Kenya is becoming more and more modern, it's still a country where women aren't as valued as men."

Talia bristled. "Maybe because they haven't stood up for themselves. The village women are taking strides in that direction."

Jim's eyes narrowed. "And what came of it? I understand they were raided during the middle of their little meeting last night, putting them and their children in danger."

Jim was right. The women had taken a stand, but the danger was real.

"They're trying," Talia said. She lifted her chin. "What brings you out this morning?"

"Just checking on my neighbor. It's past time. I'm sure Michael would have wanted me to take a more active role in ensuring your safety." Jim glanced around at the men assembled in the great room. "Although it appears you have guests who can more than assume the role of protector."

Harm stepped forward an inch, his arms crossed

over his chest. "We're looking out for Mrs. Ryan," he confirmed.

Jim nodded. "I'm glad to see she has someone looking out for her well-being. How long will you be here?"

"A week," Big Jake confirmed.

"A week." Jim faced Talia, his eyebrows rising. He glanced around. "What happened to your hired bodyguards?"

As much as she hated answering, Talia couldn't be rude and ignore the man's question. "I haven't been able to hire new ones since the last shooting."

Jim swept his arm to encompass the room. "And when these fine gentlemen are gone? Who will protect you from poachers or rebels?"

Talia stood straighter, her shoulders pushed back, her chin raised. "I have a gun. I know how to use it."

"If you see them coming and they don't outnumber you." Her neighbor shook his head. "Face it, Talia, you need to sell and move on with your life. This was Michael's dream, not yours."

"It was both of our dreams," Talia insisted. Something about Jim's insistence made her back teeth grind. The fact that she was a woman shouldn't have any bearing on her ability to run the resort. She'd done just fine for the past year. Only for the last couple of months had she been plagued with troubles.

Two of her guards had been killed the last time the SEALs had been her guests. She frowned. Could it be they were the draw? As quick as the thought surfaced, she put it aside. They'd been gone a couple weeks, and the troubles had continued in their absence. The local witch doctor was blaming it on her being a woman, running a resort without a man to protect her.

"For the record," Talia said, "I have no intention of selling, now or anytime in the future."

Jim held out his hand to Talia. "I understand. If you should change your mind, I'll do what I can to help you out." He tipped his head toward the men in the room, his glance lingering longer on Harm. "Nice to meet you gentlemen. I hope you enjoy your stay in Kenya before your return to duty." With that, he turned and left the lodge.

Talia followed him to the door and closed it behind him. Then she turned and leaned back against the wood paneling, letting go of the breath she'd been holding.

Harm reached for her hand. "Are you all right?"

She nodded. "It doesn't seem to matter how well I run this place, there are more doubters than supporters around here for a woman running a business alone. It makes me so angry. I'm fully capable of owning and operating this resort. I don't need a man to back me, and I don't want to sell."

"And you shouldn't feel like you have to. This is your place. No one should tell you how to run it or to leave."

"Damn right." Big Jake joined them in the front

foyer. "From all we've seen, you do a helluva job and have every reason to be proud of your accomplishments."

The other SEALs gathered around her, along with Marly and Angela.

"You're amazing, running an operation like this," Marly said. "All I had to do was fly a single airplane. You manage an entire army of people to keep this place running."

"I *used* to manage a lot of people." Talia sighed. "Lately, I can't keep them. They're bailing on me like mice on a sinking ship."

"Because of rumors and witch doctor mumbo jumbo," Angela added.

"Still, if I can't get help, I can't run this place. I might as well sell it." Talia tugged on her hand to release it from Harm's grip.

He didn't let go. "You just told Krause you weren't selling."

"And when I told him that, I meant it. At least not selling it to him."

"Why not him?"

Her cheeks heated. "He makes my teeth grind. He tried to buy the place from my husband on several occasions, but Michael refused to sell to him. He didn't trust the man."

"Why?"

She shrugged. "Gut feeling." Talia pasted a smile on her face. "So, what's on the agenda for the day? Are you certain you don't want to go on safari?"

T-Mac raised a hand. "I'm all for a beer and the swimming pool."

"I have my eyes on that hammock I saw in the garden," Diesel said. "After I call Reese."

"How's she doing back in the States?" T-Mac asked.

"She's landed another bodyguard gig. Apparently, Secretary of Defense Klein spread the word that she's one tough cookie and can handle any job, big or small."

"And how do you feel about that after your trek in the jungle?" Harm asked.

Diesel shrugged. "She'd be good, and it's what she wants to do. I'll take any time I can get with her."

"It'll be tough keeping up a relationship with both of you on disparate missions," Harm said.

"We'll make it work. I love that woman." Diesel grinned. "She's everything I didn't know I was looking for, and then some."

Talia's heart squeezed in her chest. She'd had that with Michael, and they'd been together all their married life. Until Michael died. Now, the thought of starting over with another relationship was daunting to the point of terrifying.

"What if she's injured or—God forbid—killed on the job?" Talia asked.

Diesel's lips thinned. "Then I will have had her for as long as I did and loved every minute of it. It goes both ways. I could be killed on my job and leave her alone. We both know the risks and are willing to accept them. We don't know how long we have on this earth, but we want to spend as much of that time as we can with each other."

Harm's hand tightened on Talia's.

She didn't dare glance in his direction. She wasn't sure what she'd see, nor was she sure she was ready for whatever came next between them.

For now, she had her own issues to face, dealing with the troubles at the resort. She had to focus on them, not on a potential love affair that would only end in heartbreak.

Chapter Eleven

Diesel's words hit Harm square in the chest. His teammate knew he wouldn't be able to spend much of his time with the love of his life, Reese Brantley, but he was willing to commit to her nonetheless.

Relationships for SEALs were usually doomed to failure because of the nature of the job. They were seldom home and, when they were, they were on call for whatever emergency or mission arose. They had to be ready to bug out at a moment's notice. What woman could handle that kind of uncertainty?

His hand tightened on Talia's. This was a woman who faced hardships head-on and didn't back down. She'd stood up to her neighbor when the man suggested she give up and move on. As a lone woman in what could be a hostile country, she had enough difficulties to face without being burdened with a long-distance relationship—one in which the man would rarely make it back to Kenya to see her.

Wait. What was he thinking? He wasn't considering a long-term relationship with Talia, was he?

The thought of walking away at the end of the week was looking less and less appealing. The woman had managed to crawl beneath his skin and straight through to that hardened muscle in his chest.

It wasn't so hard anymore, was it?

Like Reese was to Diesel, Talia was everything Harm hadn't known he was looking for in a woman. She was smart, tough, beautiful and loyal to the man she loved with all her heart. She'd love her husband… deeply.

Harm hadn't known he was looking for someone who could love so hard and fiercely. But that's what he wanted. Someone like Talia.

What was he thinking? Anything between the two of them would never work. She was tied to this resort in the heart of Kenya, a world away from the place Harm called home in Virginia.

He couldn't promise her anything, and he couldn't expect her to promise him love and commitment when he wasn't sure when he'd be back in Africa again.

It was pure insanity to even think he could be with Talia. He'd have to quit the navy. Then he'd be jobless. What woman wanted a man who couldn't pull in a paycheck?

No, he'd be better off sticking to his original idea of a quick fling and leave at the end of the week. No strings. No commitment.

Still, he couldn't bring himself to release Talia's hand. In the few days he had left at the All Things

Wild Resort, he had to help Talia figure out where the threat originated and nip it in the bud. Or blow it out of the water. Whatever left her safe and made him feel better about leaving her alone.

"Buck and I are going to the village to see if anyone needs any medical attention after last night's raid," Angela said.

"I promised one of the local ranchers I'd stop by and check out his plane," Marly said.

"You're not considering buying another plane, are you?" Big Jake asked.

Pitbull chuckled. "No, she doesn't need any more target practice."

Marly elbowed him in the side. "I didn't use my plane as target practice. I couldn't let that monster get away in it and continue dealing in exotic animals and human trafficking. My choices were let him go free or sacrifice my plane." She lifted her chin. "As far as I was concerned, there was no choice. I saw some of the animals and women he'd stolen. He was a monster. Blowing up my plane was a small price to pay for ridding this planet of that scum."

"And you did the right thing." Pitbull kissed her and hugged her close. "I know how much that plane meant to you."

"Damn right." She kissed him back.

Pitbull hooked an arm around her and faced the others. "And I'm going with Marly today. Unless you need me to pound on some poachers."

Talia laughed. "I wish we could find them and

let you pound on them. Unfortunately, they always manage to slip away before we can nail them with the goods."

"What about you, Big Jake?" Harm asked. "Are you hanging out here? Or do you want to ride with us into the village to do some questioning?"

"I think I'll tag along with you. I'm interested in finding out who busted up your party last night."

"Great." T-Mac headed for the door. "Call if you need backup. Otherwise, you can find me at the pool."

"I left my weapon in my room. I'll be ready to go in a few minutes," Big Jake said and sprinted up the stairs.

The great room slowly cleared of everyone except Talia and Harm.

"What do you need help with first?" he asked.

"I need you to enjoy your vacation," she said. "I can handle things on my own."

He held up his hand. "You might as well save your breath. I'm sticking to you like a fly to flypaper. We need to get to the village to question the ladies about who crashed their party."

"I have to take care of things around here first. Give me an hour and I'll be ready to go to the village." She marched into the dining room and frowned.

"Looking for the dishes?" Harm asked from behind her.

Talia frowned. "Well, yes."

"The guys cleaned up after themselves, washed and put away their dishes." Harm chuckled. "They might be hard to house-train, but they're familiar with KP."

"KP?" Talia asked.

"Kitchen patrol." Harm followed Talia into the kitchen, where the chef was pulling a roast out of the oven.

The scent of roast and seasonings filled the air and made Harm's mouth water.

"Um." Talia sniffed the air. "That smells wonderful."

"I made it for lunch," Jamba said. "The men can make sandwiches, or I can cook a pot of rice and make gravy."

"Sandwiches will be fine," Harm said. "They won't care, as long as it's easy and satisfying."

"Good, then I'll help clean cabins and make beds," the chef offered.

"Don't," Talia said. "I've got that covered."

Harm shook his head. "The guys assured me they made their own beds. They won't need service in their rooms or cabins."

"But they'll want fresh towels," Talia insisted.

Harm shook his head. "They're all about reusing and saving the environment. They can use them one more time, and then we'll gather them and bring them to the laundry room tomorrow."

Talia tapped a finger to her chin, the frown still in place. "That doesn't leave much for me to do."

"Good." He touched her arm. "Then we can get into the village and find out who's behind the troubles."

"Yeah, about that," she said. "I've been asking around for the past couple of weeks and have yet to locate the instigator."

"You have me to help now." He held up his hands. "Not that you couldn't do it on your own. Woman power and all. I'm just saying two heads could be better than one on this effort."

She laughed. "All right, then. Give me a minute to check on the truck—"

He grinned. "I had Marly and Pitbull install the starter this morning before breakfast. It's running like a champ."

Talia's lips twisted into a wry grin. "You've thought of everything."

"I try." He held out his arm. "Ready?"

Her eyes narrowed. "I'm not sure."

"Not sure about what?" he asked, all innocence and charm.

"Not sure I trust you." But she hooked her hand through his arm anyway.

"What's not to trust?" He winked and led her through the kitchen door to the front entrance.

Big Jake met them there and followed them out to the truck.

Harm offered to drive but said it would tie up his shooting hand if he did. Jake did the same, so Talia took the wheel. The truck behaved itself and started right up. The drive into the village was bless-edly uneventful.

By all appearances, nothing untoward had oc-curred the night before. The bonfire in the middle of the square had been reduced to a pile of ashes. Small children scampered between the huts, crying out in excitement. Mothers worked over smaller cooking fires, wove baskets or pieced together beadwork for sale to the tourists. If Harm didn't know better, he'd think it was just another day in rural Kenya.

Talia parked the truck on the edge of the village.

Big Jake got out and headed one direction while Talia and Harm went another.

His pistol tucked beneath his light jacket, Harm took Talia's hand as they walked into the center of the buildings.

Talia greeted several of the women and knelt to hug a couple children. She appeared to be looking for someone. After a few minutes, she leaned into Harm. "I don't see Eriku."

"And we haven't asked about the events of last evening," he reminded her in a quiet voice only she could hear.

Beneath her breath, she answered, "I'm sensing the women are a little more closed off than usual."

"How so?"

"Normally, they rush to greet me and ask how things are at the resort. They used to all want to work for me. But now…" She shook her head. "I feel like they will shut down altogether if I start asking questions."

"Then let me," Harm said. He started toward one of the elderly women who squatted on her haunches over a cooking pot, stirring the contents slowly.

"Excuse me, ma'am," Harm started.

She glanced up at him through glazed eyes with a disturbing white film over her pupils. Was she blind? If so, she wouldn't have seen anything that had happened the night before.

Already committed to conversing with the woman, Harm was shocked when she cleared her throat and said, "Eriku is not here. She went with Jolani to the preserve because she'd heard poachers were after the elephants for their tusks. If she is killed…" Her rheumy gaze shot to Talia, who was walking toward Harm. "Why did you have to turn Eriku against her own people?"

"What do you mean? I didn't turn her against her own people," Talia said. She squatted on her haunches beside the older woman. "She learned what was happening to her country, to the animals in Kenya and all of Africa. She decided to do something about it."

"We were happy before you and your husband arrived. We were not fighting among ourselves." A frown deepened the grooves across the woman's forehead. "Now, you will cost us the lives of our young people, our children and our men."

Talia sighed. "I'm not the one poaching. Nor am

I the one attacking your people like last night. I'm as much a victim as the women and children were last night."

"But the men wouldn't have attacked if you had not come to the village," the old lady insisted. "It's you. Gakuru is right. A lone woman can't run a resort. It creates bad juju. Nothing has been right since your husband died. You must leave before our village loses anyone else."

"Anyone else? Who have you lost?"

The old woman's lips clamped shut, and she turned away from Talia.

Talia straightened. Harm cupped her elbow and led her away from the crotchety old villager. "Don't listen to her. You didn't cause the problems around here. The poachers know what they are doing is illegal. Someone would eventually catch them in the act. The fact that you turned them over to the sheriff isn't a reflection on you making life worse for the villagers. Their actions—killing protected species—are what's causing the rift among their people."

"I know that. But if you hear the same thing over and over, you start believing it to be true. Maybe I am bad juju."

Big Jake hurried over to them. "No one's talking or naming names of the people who attacked last night. However, the few people I spoke to all said they think Eriku is in trouble."

Talia touched Big Jake's arm. "Where did she go? Did they say?"

Harm wanted to know the same. The savanna contained a vast number of wide-open acres of grass, watering holes and massive herds of wild animals. Finding Eriku in all of that would be close to impossible without a direction to head.

Big Jake frowned. "The people I spoke with said she was heading for the elephants' favorite watering hole." His eyes narrowed. "Do you know where that is?"

Talia grinned. "I do. But we better get there in a hurry. If Eriku is there to stop the poachers, I fear she's in trouble. She won't have a weapon to protect herself, even if the poachers took the teenager seriously."

The three headed back to the truck and jumped in.

Talia spun the vehicle around and punched the accelerator to the floor, heading north toward the savanna and the elephant watering hole.

Thirty minutes stretched by in excruciating slowness, no matter that Talia had the accelerator all the way to the floor, kicking up a plume of dust behind the truck.

Harm held on to keep from being thrown into the dash or ejected from the vehicle altogether.

In the seat behind the cab, Big Jake grunted and bounced around, tossed like a rag doll on the bumpy, rutted road across the savanna.

"I assume you know where you're going?" Harm yelled over the roar of the engine and the noise of the tires hitting the ruts.

Talia nodded, her grip so tight on the steering wheel that her knuckles turned white. "I just hope we're in time to help Eriku. She shouldn't have gone out alone."

"She's with Jolani? I take it Jolani is a man?" Harm asked, his teeth rattling with the effort.

Talia nodded. "But they're no match for the poachers. They'd just as soon shoot them than have witnesses to their destruction. Foolish girl," Talia muttered and held on as the vehicle lurched violently into a hole and the steering wheel was almost jerked out of her hand.

Harm would have offered to drive, but changing drivers would slow them down, and Talia knew where she was going. He didn't.

After twenty-five minutes of being beaten up by the road, they rounded a curve in the path and emerged from a stand of trees, arriving at the edge of a large muddy pond.

A herd of zebras scattered in all directions and cape buffalo shifted from hoof to hoof, but retained their lazy stance near the life-giving liquid.

"This is the elephants' watering hole?"

Talia nodded. "They usually show up here." She sat behind the wheel, her hands still gripping it tightly.

No elephants and no Eriku in sight. "I don't know where else to look. Unless…" She stepped on the accelerator and spun the truck around, heading back to the rutted road and straight for a stand of acacia trees. "They hang out in the shade sometimes!" Talia yelled.

Harm was glad to know it, but his teeth were banging together so hard, he didn't bother to respond. He hoped they found the elephants and Eriku before he chipped his teeth down to nubs.

TALIA'S HEART RACED and her arms hurt from manhandling the steering wheel of the old pickup, heading straight for the copse of trees she'd known the elephants to retreat to when the sun got too hot. If they weren't there, she wasn't sure where she'd look to find Eriku. The girl needed to understand how dangerous it was to chase after poachers.

As she pulled into the shadows of the grove of acacia trees, she saw the huge silhouettes of elephants standing in a circle.

"Oh, no." Talia's heart sank to the pit of her belly. She slowed the vehicle and eased up to where the elephants stood, swaying slightly from foot to foot.

One of the largest of the elephants nudged at something on the ground and then raised her trunk in the air and trumpeted. The other elephants joined her, trumpeting so loud, Talia had to cover her ears.

One of the pachyderms shifted just enough that Talia could see between them to the animal lying on the ground in a pool of blood, its tusks missing, hacked out of its head.

Bile rose in Talia's throat. She swallowed hard to keep from losing it in front of the men.

Harm swore softly beside her. He'd pulled his gun from the holster beneath his light jacket and scanned the area.

Talia focused her gaze on Harm rather than on the dead elephant.

The herd gathered around their fallen member. Now silent, they paid tribute to their dead, a giant ring of solidarity in the face of the tragedy.

"We should go," Big Jake said. "Apparently, we're too late for the elephant."

"Any sign of Eriku?"

"Without getting out on foot, we can't comb the brush to search."

"It's not safe to get out," Talia said. "After what happened here, we can't guarantee that the elephants won't mistake us for the poachers who killed their friend." She shifted into Reverse and backed slowly away. The truck backfired, the sound like that of a high-powered rifle in the silence of nature.

The big elephant who'd trumpeted her sadness swung around at the sound. Seconds later, she was running toward the truck, building up to full speed.

"Go! Go! Go!" Harm shouted, holding on to the dash and the armrest.

Talia was afraid to turn around and lose the lead she had on the not-so-gentle giant, who seemed to be in a rage to trample the occupants of the truck.

Talia pressed hard on the accelerator, sending the vehicle hurtling backward. For several long seconds, she didn't think they'd get away before the elephant slammed into the front of the truck.

"We can't afford to lose this truck, too," Talia muttered, staring over her shoulder at the field of grass behind them.

"More than losing this truck, I think we can't afford to let that elephant catch up to us." Harm stared out the front of the vehicle at the monstrous pachyderm pounding the ground, racing toward them.

Judging her direction by glancing in the side mirrors, Talia blasted backward, refusing to slow down before the raging cow elephant. Though she didn't focus on the animal, Talia could see her movements in her peripheral vision. The sheer size and anger in those dark eyes had her heart thundering against her ribs and her palms sweating on the steering wheel.

Soon the elephant slowed, tiring after a mad dash across the savanna.

Talia kept going, determined to get as much distance between them and the herd as possible. When she could afford to safely turn around and drive away without being trampled, she did. And they were on their way back toward the village, tragedy averted.

Harm and Talia watched each of the side mirrors.

"She stopped running," Harm said.

"Whew!" Big Jake leaned over the seat and pounded Harm on the back. "Talia had me worried for a moment. That elephant could have stomped the crap out of this truck, with us in it." He laughed. "I never should have doubted our driver. She's amazing."

"Yes, she is." Harm reached across the cab and touched Talia's shoulder.

Talia's insides warmed until she thought again about the elephant brutally murdered by the poachers.

The killing had to stop. But first, she had to find Eriku and make sure she wasn't as much a victim as the elephant lying dead on the Kenyan savanna.

Chapter Twelve

Harm didn't like the carnage he'd witnessed. And the vision of solidarity in the pack of elephants' grief stuck with him long after he'd left the scene of the crime.

"How can people do that to an animal and call themselves human?" Big Jake asked.

"For money," Talia replied, her lips thinning. "My biggest question right now is where the hell is Eriku? If they did anything to hurt her…" Her hands tightened on the steering wheel until her knuckles turned white.

Harm held on as they bumped along the dirt road back to the lodge. "Who else would know where to find Eriku?"

Talia shook her head. "I don't know. The people in the village told us what they knew. The only people who might know are the poachers who killed the elephant."

"Where to from here?" Harm asked.

"Back to the lodge. I need to call in the park

rangers to document and investigate the kill. This can't continue."

The ride back to the lodge was considerably slower than the ride to the elephant watering hole, but still bumpy. Harm held on to keep from being thrown from the open-sided truck.

They arrived after noon. No sooner had they pulled into the compound than the other four members of the SEAL team emerged from the lodge, along with Marly and Angela.

Harm hurried around to the driver's side of the truck, but Talia had already slipped from her seat onto the ground.

"Did you find Eriku?" Angela asked.

Talia shook her head. "No. But we found another dead animal."

"Another rhino?" Buck guessed.

T-Mac stepped up beside Buck. "Or was it an elephant?"

Harm's eyes narrowed. "What makes you think it was an elephant this time?"

"Buck and Angela said you'd gotten word from the villagers that Eriku had gone out to stop poachers at the elephant watering hole." T-Mac's jaw tightened. "But that's not the only reason I guessed elephant. You have to see what I found online."

Harm's gut knotted. "What?"

"Just come inside and see. It might be a coincidence, or it might have some bearing on what's going on around here."

Harm reached for Talia's hand and followed T-Mac into the lodge. He caught up with Diesel and leaned close. "Do you know what he's talking about?"

Diesel shook his head. "It's a mystery to me. T-Mac's been holed up in the study since he came in from his swim. Can't keep that man away from computers for long."

All he could figure was that T-Mac had found something on the internet, but he couldn't imagine it would help them resolve what was happening in Kenya. The troubles there were deeper and more prevalent than a SEAL team on vacation could eradicate in the few days they had left there.

T-Mac sat in the chair behind the desk and ran his fingers across the keyboard.

The rest of the SEAL team, Marly, Angela and Talia crowded around him as an image appeared on the monitor. In the middle of the screen was a rhinoceros lying on its side. A man with a rifle stood with his foot on the animal's neck. The proud hunter had killed the animal and was posing over his dead conquest. The rhino was intact, still in possession of its two horns.

A collective gasp rose from everyone in the room.

"That could be an old photograph," Talia suggested.

"I looked up the stats on it. It was posted yesterday."

"Still, it could be an old photo," Angela said.

"I thought of that, too, but look here." T-Mac enlarged the image and pointed to the hindquarters of the rhino. A distinctive scar could clearly be seen. A scar exactly like the one on the rhino they'd found dead the day before.

Talia cursed beneath her breath. "If what I'm seeing is true, the poachers didn't kill the rhino. They only scavenged what was left." She lifted the telephone. "I need to report this to the park rangers. They need to know someone is illegally hunting on protected land."

"Wait, you'll want to see this." T-Mac clicked a few keys, and another image appeared.

This time it wasn't a rhinoceros lying on the ground. It was a larger animal. Again, a hunter stood with a big rifle, his foot on the neck of the dead animal. The dead elephant still had its tusks.

"This photograph was posted last night." T-Mac glanced toward Harm. "Was that your dead elephant you found today?"

"We didn't get close enough to identify specific details," Harm admitted. "Its friends were gathered around and didn't like being interrupted in their grief."

"Who posted the pictures?" Talia demanded.

"I'm working on that," T-Mac said. "I can trace it back to an IP address. If you give me a little more time, I might be able to get the name of the owner of that IP address."

"Get it." Talia lifted the telephone and punched

numbers on the keypad before she looked up again. "The more ammunition we have to give the rangers, the better off they'll be in locating the hunter and the outfitter who brought him to the preserve to kill."

Talia gave the information to the Kenya Wildlife Service and promised to be available to answer any further questions and take them out to the site when they could send a ranger. When she hung up the phone, she appeared tired and disheartened. "Why can't people understand these animals are a finite quantity? The more they kill, the fewer there will be until they become extinct." She jabbed a finger toward the man in the image. "And I'll bet that man is educated, has a degree and probably a lot of money. He, of all people, should know what his sport is costing the world." She backed away. "I'm sorry. This isn't your problem. I have to keep reminding myself you all are here on vacation. You shouldn't be burdened with our issues." She turned and walked away.

Harm's heart squeezed hard in his chest.

"She doesn't understand that this is what we do," Diesel said. "We fight for what's right."

"I don't know about you, but I feel like punching someone," Pitbull said. "Namely, the guy in that picture."

"You and me both," Buck said. "He can't be too far from here, if we're finding his trophies." He leaned over T-Mac's shoulder. "There has to be some connection to this area."

"I'm working on it," T-Mac said. "Like I said, it takes time."

"Well, we might not have time. He could be out there now taking aim at another animal."

"We have to find him before he succeeds," Big Jake said.

"Exactly," Diesel agreed. "And we have to find whoever is leading him there."

Big Jake shook his head slowly, his eyes sad. "You should have seen those other elephants. It was downright heartbreaking the way they rallied around their fallen comrade."

The other occupants of the room fell silent.

Harm heard all their comments, but his gaze followed Talia from the room. She was in a bad spot with what was happening. If she called the wildlife service every time an animal died, soon the rangers would be camped in their area, which would put a damper on the killing and on whoever was leading the hunts. Harm would bet there was a lot of money paid out to go on one of those hunts. And money was a huge motivator. People would kill for money. Sometimes not even a lot of money.

Could it be the troubles Talia was having were all motivated by money?

Harm would like to question the witch doctor in the village. What if someone was paying him to scare Talia away from the resort? Paying off a witch doctor had to be a drop in the bucket compared to the amount a rich hunter might pay for a chance to bag exotic game.

Harm followed Talia across the great room and into the kitchen. She had to be hurting and scared for Eriku.

He wanted to take away her pain and help her in any way he could. She was in danger, and they had yet to resolve who was at the root of the problem. The end of the week loomed, seeming to speed toward him. How could he leave her when his time there was up?

TALIA WAS GOING through the motions of running the resort. She had rooms to clean, guests to see to and meals to plan. None of these things took the edge off her worry for Eriku. The teen had likely stepped into the middle of a hot spot. Poachers were ruthless and wouldn't hesitate to kill a girl bent on shutting down their operation.

And she couldn't begin to guess how ruthless the man leading hunters to the kill was. Her stomach roiled at the images of the rhino and the elephant running through her mind, like a film reel stuck on replay.

Jamba was at the stove, stirring something in a pot. The aroma made Talia's belly tighten and growl. They'd missed lunch while out on the savanna.

"Roast's warming in the oven," Jamba said. "But if you wait an hour, dinner will be ready early."

"Thanks, Jamba." Talia turned to Harm. "Would you like to split half a roast beef sandwich?"

"Only if you let me make it. I'm sure you have a dozen things you need to be doing."

She smiled. "I'm tired just thinking about all the things I should be doing."

"Then sit and let me make the sandwich. I might not be the best cook, but give me bread and meat and I can make a mean snack." He winked and led her to the industrial-style table in the corner of the kitchen and pressed her into a chair. "Sit for a minute. You did all the hard work driving today."

She started to rise. "Yeah, but I was sitting then."

He pressed his hand on her shoulder. "And it took a lot of muscle to manhandle that truck through all those ruts. You could probably beat any one of us in arm wrestling."

She laughed. "Not hardly."

He opened the refrigerator and retrieved a bottle of water, unscrewed the cap and set it on the table in front of her. "Hydrate."

Talia popped a salute. "Yes, sir." But she took the bottle and downed half of it before she took another breath. She hadn't realized how thirsty she was until Harm had set the chilled bottle in front of her. "Thank you."

"You're welcome." With her directing, he collected lettuce, tomatoes, mayonnaise and mustard and set them on the counter. Then he sliced off two thick slices of the homemade bread Jamba baked daily and pulled the roast from the warming oven.

Talia sat mesmerized by his every move.

Harm had shed his jacket, working now in a T-shirt that was stretched taut over his chest and arms. Every move caused his muscles to flex, every sinew well defined beneath his smooth skin.

Talia couldn't help comparing Harm to her late husband. Michael had been lean and strong, but not bulky. He'd been a running back in the United States and he walked a lot in Kenya, but he hadn't been as well built as Harm. Every time Harm touched her, she could feel the sheer strength in his fingers. If he wanted, he could crush her in his grip. But he didn't. He was very careful not to hurt her. For such a big guy, he was gentle and considerate of her every need.

By the time Harm finished making the sandwich and cutting it in half, she was very hungry. But not for food. Along with her desire came a healthy dose of guilt. Was she being unfaithful to her husband's memory by lusting after another man under the roof she'd shared with Michael?

Michael wouldn't have wanted her to spend the rest of her life alone, but had she mourned him long enough? How long was long enough? Judging by the fact that she was questioning the length of time one should mourn, was it a clear indication she was ready to move on?

Harm placed the two sandwich halves on small

plates and carried them to the table. He grinned at her and sat directly opposite her.

His grin made her feel warm and liquid all over. If she'd been standing, her knees would have wobbled, suddenly boneless.

He lifted his sandwich and waited for her to take hers. "I hope you like mustard and mayo."

"Love them both." Talia held up her snack. "Thanks."

"Don't thank me until you try it. Could be the worst thing ever."

She bit into the moist roast beef, slathered in mustard and mayo. The explosion of flavors filled her mouth and she moaned. "Mmm." With her mouth too full to voice her opinion, she chewed and swallowed first. "Amazing."

"In a good way?" he asked.

"In the best way." She pushed aside her feelings of guilt and basked in the intimacy of sharing a sandwich with a sexy SEAL.

For a few minutes, they ate in silence. Then Harm asked, "Who do you know around here who runs a hunting outfit?"

She shook her head. "No one. It's illegal to hunt endangered animals. Especially when they're on a national reserve."

"What other groups offer safari treks?" Harm asked between bites of his sandwich.

"There are several resorts like All Things Wild. Tourism is big business in Africa. There's the Campfire Adventurers, African Explorers, Go Africa and other smaller outfitters like Krause Tours, us, Heart of Africa Safaris..." She smiled. "I could go on."

Harm held up a hand. "No. No. I get the idea. There are a lot of outfitters leading safaris in Kenya." He shook his head. "I guess I didn't realize how big the business was."

"All you have to do is go online and key in 'African safaris in Kenya' and you'll be overwhelmed."

"Remind me to thank Marly for recommending you. I could get stressed just by the overwhelming number of outfitters to choose from."

"Exactly." Talia finished her sandwich and gathered their plates. "Since none of my cleaning staff came in today, I need to pull laundry duty." She held up her hand. "And no, you can't help. You've already waited on me for lunch. I won't let you enter the laundry room."

"In that case, I'll check out what T-Mac's looking at. Do you want me to head to the village and ask around about Eriku?"

Talia shook her head. "If they'd known anything, they would have told me."

"Even given the bad juju you supposedly have?" He smiled, dulling the hit.

With a wry twist of her lips, she sighed. "You're right. They could have sent me on a wild goose chase this morning, just to get rid of me."

"But you did find evidence of poaching."

She nodded, a frown pushing her brow downward.

"I just hope Eriku is okay." Talia squared her shoulders. "In the meantime, I've got work to do. Help yourself to anything else you might want to eat or drink. I'll be back in the kitchen in time to set the table for dinner."

Talia would rather have stayed with Harm, but the more she was around him, the more she wanted to be with him. The end of the week would arrive before she knew it, and she'd find herself lonely and wishing he'd never left. She'd be better off weaning herself off his company before she got too used to having him around.

AN HOUR AND a half, two loads of towels, three loads of sheets and a shower later, she returned to the kitchen, her cheeks warm from the laundry room. The table had been set with cutlery, plates and glasses, and the SEALs were gathered in the kitchen trying to help but only getting in Jamba's way.

"Shoo," Talia said. "Jamba is a master chef and needs his space to prepare such wonderful dishes." She sniffed the pot on the stove. "What are we having tonight?"

"Roast lamb shank and my special sauce, potatoes au gratin and brussels sprouts," Jamba replied. "And I made a special dessert of cherries jubilee and homemade ice cream."

"I'm for skipping right to dessert," Buck announced.

"Out." Angela herded him toward the door. "You

heard the lady. Jamba needs his space to prepare his culinary delights."

Buck kissed her on the lips and grinned. "Yes, ma'am. I'm going."

The rest of the SEALs and Marly exited the kitchen, all except Harm.

Talia's heart warmed. In the short time she'd been away from him, he hadn't been out of her thoughts for a moment. "You, too."

"I'm here to carry food to the table. We can't expect you and Jamba to handle everything."

"Yes. You. Can." She drew in a deep breath and let it out. "Don't you understand? You're the guest, for heaven's sake."

"What you don't understand is that we don't mind helping. In fact, putting us to work keeps us out of trouble." He raised his brows, a smile tugging at the corners of his lips. "And let me tell you, those guys can get into trouble if they don't have something to keep them busy." He jabbed a thumb to his chest. "Including me."

Jamba set the lamb shank on a platter, sliced through the meat, poured his special sauce over it and handed the platter to Harm. "If you want to be useful, take this to the table."

Harm took the platter and smiled at Talia as if to say, *See, I told you so.* Then he marched into the dining room to the loud cheers of his friends.

Talia stared after him, shaking her head.

"You like him, don't you?" Jamba said.

Jerked back to reality and the kitchen, Talia responded automatically, "I don't know what you're talking about."

"I might be older than you, but I'm not blind. You like that one." Jamba indicated Harm with a lift of his chin. "It is possible to fall in love again, you know."

Talia's cheeks burned as she busied herself pulling the dinner rolls out of the oven and placing them in a basket. "Who said I was falling in love again?"

"You loved your husband, but he's gone. A beautiful woman like you can't go through the rest of her life alone. If you find love, you should go after it."

"I have my life here. Anyone I might love would have to be willing to stay here and work like a dog to keep this place running. A man would have to be a fool to sign up for that kind of punishment."

Jamba chuckled. "Men have been known to be fools in love."

Talia cast a sideways glance at the chef. "Including you?"

He shrugged. "I, too, have been in love."

"You?" she asked, too stunned to hold back. When she realized it might have sounded rude, she added, "When?"

He turned off the burner on the stove, poured the brussels sprouts into a bowl and carried them to the door of the kitchen. He paused before leaving the room and said, "I fell in love with a woman at culinary school. But she was heading one way and I was coming home."

"And you wish you'd followed her?" Talia asked, her gaze softening.

He nodded. "Sometimes I wonder if she'd still be interested." Then he pushed through the door and left Talia standing in the kitchen, her heart hammering against her ribs as she caught a glimpse of Harm laughing with his friends. What would it be like to give up everything she'd worked for and dare to start over?

The door closed between the kitchen and the dining room. Was it an omen? If she waited too long to go after what she wanted, would the door close on the possibility?

She slipped her hands into oven mitts, pulled the potatoes out of the oven and carried them into the dining room. As she crossed the threshold, her cheeks burned again and her heart thundered against her ribs. She felt like she was standing on the edge of a precipice. Should she back away, or jump?

Throughout the meal, she remained quiet, afraid she'd blurt out something stupid, like declaring her undying love for a man she'd only known a short time. The thought left her tongue paralyzed and she refused to look up, lest Harm see her thoughts reflected in her eyes.

By the time dinner and dessert had been consumed, Talia's insides were tied in a knot and she couldn't think, other than to offer the guests an afterdinner drink and the use of the game room. Then she excused herself, claiming a headache, and ran for her room.

As she strode through her bedroom, she passed by the photograph on the nightstand of her and Michael standing in front of the first truck they'd purchased and had modified to conduct the photography safaris. They'd been so proud of their accomplishments. They'd worked hard, investing sweat equity into cleaning up the old resort that had been established in the late 1960s. Michael had purchased the place for a song, convinced the old safari hunts would be better served as hunting for good shots—as in camera angles, not bullets.

Not all of the neighboring outfitters had been happy about their attempt to educate the tourists on the dangers of hunting the animals into extinction. Some still had the ability to purchase the right to hunt certain game, if they paid enough money to the right government officials. Those kinds of hunts had been outlawed in Kenya. But some said they still happened.

Talia lifted the photo frame and stared down at the smiling image of Michael, eight years younger and full of passion for the animals, his work and life in general. He'd been an amazing man.

She still missed him, but the pain of loss had faded to a dull ache. Up until a few weeks ago, Talia had been going through the motions, living one day to the next, as if in a fog. When the navy SEALs arrived, all that changed.

Those men had seen the horrors of war, had suffered the loss of their brothers in arms and continued to live life to the fullest. When things had gotten rough at the resort, they hadn't run in the opposite direction. They'd jumped in and attacked the problem. She admired their resilience and determination. They'd inspired her to pull her head out of the haze of her own loss and get on with life and living.

Maybe she was on the rebound from Michael's death, or tired of being lonely, but there was something there when she touched Harm. Something she'd never expected to feel again. That sense of wonder in a new relationship. The hope she'd felt when she was younger. That hope of finding the love of her life, that someone she could share her hopes and dreams with. Someone she could come home to and grow old with.

But Harm had been very clear with her. He was interested in a physical relationship, nothing else. Somewhere along the line of his life, he'd been hurt by a woman, causing him to be cautious when committing or giving his heart.

Talia suspected the man was holding back, maybe even lying to himself. Otherwise, he wouldn't have gone to the trouble of fixing breakfast for the two of them to share in bed. He'd have ditched her and gone down to eat at the table with his buddies.

But he'd chosen to come back to her. And he'd had the opportunity to make love to her again, and opted out to give her time to dress and be ready for her duties as hostess. If he'd been that interested in a physical relationship only, wouldn't he have taken her up on her offer of her body before breakfast?

Talia realized she was thinking of making love to Harm while she held a photograph of herself and her late husband.

A surge of guilt washed over her, making her stomach roil and her chest hurt. She could never forget how much she'd loved Michael and wished he was still there to share all of life's joys and challenges with her.

But the fact was, he was gone, and she had to find her new normal. She wasn't old enough to be put out to pasture. And, as Harm had pointed out, she wasn't too old to start over. Maybe fall in love again and have those children she'd put off because she and Michael had been too busy saving the animals to think of themselves or anyone else who might come along.

Talia reached out to touch Michael's face, only to come into contact with the cold, hard glass covering the image. Michael was gone. Talia had no other option but to continue living, breathing and making decisions that only involved her.

But to fall in love? With a stranger? No way. Jamba was wrong. Falling in love couldn't happen that fast. She'd dated Michael for several months before she knew he was the one for her. He'd been her best friend before he'd become her lover and then her husband.

With Harm, he'd gone straight from stranger to the person she lusted after. Successful relationships weren't founded on such shaky structure. They needed mutual understanding and respect, as well as time to get to know each other.

Harm was only there for a few more days. Why start something that could only be short term?

Talia ducked into the shower and rinsed off. Though she'd showered the dust of the savanna off her body earlier, she felt the need to cool her skin. Since before dinner, she'd alternated between cool and hot. She'd begun to wonder if she'd started early menopause with the accompanying hot flashes. But each time she got hot, she could trace the temperature increase to thoughts about Harm or glances exchanged with the man.

Yes, a cool shower might go a long way to restoring her balance.

Afterward, she slipped into a lightweight silk nightgown. Still overheated by the relentless fantasies swirling in her head, she dimmed the lights and stepped through the French doors leading out onto her balcony. The cool night breeze brushed across her skin, calming her when nothing else seemed to do the trick.

The sound of a door opening and closing in the room beside hers made her jump and pushed her pulse into overdrive again. Harm's room shared the balcony with Talia's. If she really didn't want to see the man, she'd step back into her room and close her door.

But something made her stand her ground and stare out at the night. A shooting star flashed across the dark sky. Talia found herself making a wish. A wish for happiness. Whether it meant living her life alone at the resort...or falling in love with someone else...well, she left the wish open-ended. Let the chips fall where they would.

The French door from the room next to hers opened and Harm stepped out on the balcony. At first, he didn't see her standing there, giving Talia a moment to study him in the light from the room behind him.

He'd removed his shirt and stood in his jeans, barefoot.

Talia's mouth went dry and she swept her tongue across her lips.

"How long have you been standing there?" he asked without turning toward her. His warm, husky tone seeped into her skin like melted chocolate.

She gulped, heat filling her face and traveling south to pool in her core. "I was here before you."

Then he turned and opened his arms.

Talia didn't hesitate—she closed the distance between then and melted into his embrace. Who was she trying to kid by thinking she could ignore him until he left? This was where she'd longed to be all day. In this man's arms, pressed to his chest and all other parts of his body.

He pressed his lips to the top of her head. "I've wanted to do that since before I got out of bed this morning."

She laughed and wrapped her arms around his waist. "I am afraid…" she admitted.

"Afraid?" He leaned back and stared down at her. "Of me?"

She shook her head, staring up into dark eyes reflecting the light from the moon. "Of me."

"Explain that so a mere man might understand. Please." He tipped her chin up and brushed his mouth across hers in a featherlight kiss.

"I was afraid that the more time I was with you, the more I'd want to be with you. Then when you're gone, I… I didn't want to think about that." She sucked in a breath and let it go. "You're only here a few days. I didn't want to get too attached."

He gave her a lopsided grin. "I guess I understand. We live worlds apart. It doesn't make sense to start something we can't finish."

Talia nodded, her eyes stinging with red-hot tears she refused to let fall. "No sense at all."

He kissed her again, just enough to tease her and make her want more. "Do you want me to leave?" he asked, his breath smelling of cherries jubilee and sweet vanilla ice cream.

She'd be smart to tell him to go.

"No. Please, stay."

A cool breeze made Talia shiver. Or was it in anticipation of what might come next?

Harm rubbed his hands over her arms. "Are you cold?"

She lifted one shoulder. "A little," she lied. Why tell him he made her shiver with longing? He'd think she was desperate. And she was. Desperate for him to run his hands over her body, to make her feel alive all over again.

Harm captured her cheeks in his hands and guided her face up to his. Then he claimed her mouth, pushing his tongue past her teeth to tangle with hers in a kiss so deep and profound, it left her weak in the knees and trembling.

"You are cold," he whispered against her lips. Then he bent, scooped her up into his arms and carried her into his room, kicking the door closed behind him.

Talia wrapped her arm around his neck and leaned into the hard muscles of his chest. She loved that he carried her as if she weighed nothing. He didn't groan or break a sweat as he strode across the room and laid her on the bed.

She stared up at him as his hands reached for the button on his jeans.

Again, she ran her tongue across her dry lips. "Protection?"

A slow, sexy smile slipped across his mouth. "Got

it." He nodded toward the nightstand, where a foil packet lay.

Her pulse quickened. Had he come to bed with bedding her in mind? Her belly tightened, and warmth spread from her core outward. She sat up and helped him push the button loose on his jeans.

Then they were falling into the bed naked, kissing, touching and holding each other in a frantic attempt to get as close as possible. They came together in a hot, dynamic, pulsing explosion of lust.

After her pulse returned to normal, she lay against Harm's side, basking in the afterglow.

"I could get used to having you lying naked beside me," Harm admitted.

Talia trailed a finger over his hard chest. "Wouldn't you get tired of a purely physical relationship?"

He chuckled. "I think we've gone past that."

She leaned up on her elbow. "I thought you didn't want anything else."

He smoothed the hair out of her face and tucked it behind her ear. "I was wrong. You make me want more."

Her heart swelled as she sank into the curve of his arm.

He tightened his hold on her, his hand sliding across her bare skin. "I want you for more than just the sex."

"Why?" Talia demanded.

"You're smart, strong and determined." He kissed

her temple. "In my line of work, I need a woman who can hold her own when I'm away." He slipped his arm from beneath her and leaned over her. "I need a woman who doesn't need me."

"That doesn't make sense," she said, her voice breathless, her heart pounding.

"I need a woman who wants to be with me, but who can function on her own." He kissed her forehead, her nose and finally her lips. "I need you."

"I don't need you," Talia said. "But I want you."

"Exactly."

Then she shook her head. "But that wouldn't be true. I find myself needing you, the more time I spend with you." She lifted her head and pressed her lips to his.

"We are a mess, aren't we?" Harm claimed her lips with his.

Then they were making love all over again, in a fevered frenzy. Hot, hard and passionate, as if neither could get enough of the other.

When Talia had temporarily slaked her thirst for Harm, she drifted to sleep, happy for the first time in long time and hopeful of the future.

A few hours later, she awoke, thirsty. Not for making love again, quite yet, but really thirsty.

"What's wrong?" Harm asked, his voice gritty with sleep.

"Nothing. I'm going down for some water. Do you want anything from the kitchen?" she asked.

"No, thank you." He lay with his arm over his

eyes. "I think you sucked every bone out of my body. I can't even move to turn off the light."

She laughed and rolled out of the bed.

He moved his arm, opening his eyes long enough to rake her body with his gaze. "You're beautiful. You know that?"

She slid her nightgown over her head and stepped into her panties. "No, but I do now. Mind if I borrow one of your shirts? Or would you rather I went to my room and got my robe?"

"Take my shirt hanging in the wardrobe," he said and closed his eyes. "Let me go get that drink for you."

"No. You stay put. I'll only be a moment." She pulled on his long-sleeved shirt and padded barefoot from the room, closing the door softly behind her. She didn't want to wake Big Jake, though she wasn't sure their lovemaking had been all that quiet. Big Jake could be awake at that moment, cringing.

Her footsteps were so soft, she couldn't hear them herself as she tiptoed down the staircase and out to the kitchen. Once she had a bottle of chilled water in her hand, she headed out into the hallway. The front door of the lodge stood ajar. Thinking perhaps Mr. Wiggins, the leopard, had nudged the door open, she poked her head through the door and glanced out into the night. "Mr. Wiggins?" she called out softly.

The sound unique to the leopard came from close to the steps leading up onto the front porch. He sounded stressed, possibly in pain.

Her heartbeat kicking up a notch, Talia hurried out onto the deck and down the steps. "Mr. Wiggins? Where are you, sweetie?"

Again, the animal called out to her. This time she determined the sound came from the corner of the lodge, near the bushes rimming the porch.

She ran barefoot across the grass and around the side of the building, where she almost tripped over the leopard.

Mr. Wiggins lay on his side. He didn't get up and wrap himself around her legs as was his usual greeting. Instead, he lay still, barely lifting his head to stare up at her in the starlight.

"Hey, big guy." She knelt beside him and laid the bottle of water on the grass. "What's wrong?"

He gave his deep-throated rumble that turned breathy on the end, and he coughed.

Talia rubbed her hand over his neck. "Are you sick? Did you get hurt?" She ran her hands over his body, but couldn't find any sign of injury. She'd worked with sick animals before, but she didn't have any idea what might be wrong with the big cat. "Wait here, I'll get help." She straightened and was about to turn back to the house when something hard and heavy hit her on the back of the head.

Before she could make a sound, the stars blinked out and she sank to the ground, the sound of Mr. Wiggins's rumbling growl the last thing she heard.

Chapter Thirteen

Sated from making love into the wee hours of the morning, Harm must have fallen asleep. When he woke, the gray light of early morning edged in around the curtains over the French door.

He stretched and reached for Talia. The bed beside him was empty, the pillow dented from where she'd been sleeping. She must have gotten up early. Harm hadn't even felt her come back to bed after getting a drink from the kitchen. The woman could slip in and out of a room making very little noise.

He climbed out of the bed, pulled on jeans and dragged a T-shirt over his head before he left his room in search of Talia.

Knowing her, she was probably in the kitchen, helping Jamba start breakfast for her guests.

Padding barefoot down the stairs, Harm paused in the foyer and stared at the front door, which was open.

The door was never left open.

A trickle of apprehension slithered across his skin,

raising gooseflesh. He walked outside onto the porch and looked around.

A beat-up old truck rumbled up to the lodge and parked near the corner of the house. Jamba pushed his large frame out of the driver's seat and stood, stretching in the morning light as the sun eased up over the horizon. He gave Harm a friendly wave and then frowned. Jamba hurried toward the bushes and squatted on his haunches.

Harm walked to the edge of the porch, curious as to what Jamba was staring at. There appeared to be something lying on the ground.

"Mr. Payne!" Jamba straightened and waved Harm over. "Mr. Wiggins is not well."

Harm jogged to where Jamba hovered over the resort mascot, the long, spotted leopard Talia had named Mr. Wiggins. The animal lay on its side, taking short, shallow breaths.

"What do you suppose is wrong with him?" Jamba asked.

Harm ran his hand over the cat, searching for an injury and not finding anything obvious. "I don't know. He seems to be in some kind of respiratory distress."

"What's going on?" Buck called out from the cabin he shared with Angela.

"The leopard's down. We don't know why," Harm answered.

Angela leaned through the door. "Want me to take a look at him?"

"Yes," Harm said. "He doesn't look well at all."

"I'll be right there." Angela ducked back inside the cabin and came out a minute later, dressed and carrying her doctor's satchel.

Diesel, T-Mac, Pitbull and Marly wandered out of their cabins and gathered around the leopard. Big Jake came out on the porch. "What's going on?"

"The big cat is down," Diesel said. "Has anyone told Talia?"

"Big Jake, could you get Talia?" Angela called out. "She needs to know what's going on. I'm not sure I can be of any help. I'm a human doctor, not a veterinarian."

"I'll get her." He ran back inside. A couple minutes later, he was back on the porch. "She's not here."

Harm's heart skidded to a halt. "What do you mean, not here?"

He shook his head. "She's not anywhere in the lodge. I looked everywhere."

About that time, Harm noticed something lying at the base of a nearby bush. His gut clenched and he sucked in a harsh breath. Then he bent to retrieve a plastic bottle of water that had never been opened.

"What did you find?" T-Mac asked.

Harm couldn't tear his gaze off what he held in his hand. "A bottle of water."

T-Mac chuckled. "Do you suppose the cat went for a bottle of water and was on his way back to bed when he took ill?"

Realization dawned on him, spreading like a

brushfire through his consciousness. "Talia went downstairs for a drink of water," he said softly.

T-Mac's smile slipped. "When?"

Harm pushed his empty hand through his hair. "I don't know. I must have fallen asleep. It was maybe a couple of hours ago." He looked around at the cabins and the main lodge.

Big Jake put the team to work. "Diesel and Pitbull, check the outbuildings. Buck and T-Mac, go through the entire lodge from top to bottom. I believe there's a wine cellar and an attic. Make sure I didn't miss anything. Harm and I will check the truck, the grounds around the cabins and out toward the landing strip."

"Find Talia," Harm said. He could kick himself for not going down to the kitchen for the water. At the very least, he should have gone with her.

Big Jake stared at the bottle of water. "She probably came out to check on the cat."

"If she did, where is she now?" Harm asked. He took off at a run, circling the cabin, calling out her name. "Talia! Talia!"

He checked the truck where they'd parked it the day before. Talia wasn't in it. Even more disturbing, she hadn't taken it. After checking the grounds all the way out to the landing strip where Marly had landed her plane the last time they were at the resort, he was all-out alarmed. He ran all the way back to the resort, where he met up with Big Jake.

"Anything?" Harm asked.

Big Jake shook his head. "Nothing."

The others all converged on the lodge's sweeping veranda, each reporting he'd found nothing.

"We need to get Mr. Wiggins to a vet," Angela said. "Marly and I will do that while you guys find Talia. She wouldn't want us to leave the animal in this shape." She glanced around, caught Jamba's attention. "Could we borrow your truck to get Mr. Wiggins to the nearest veterinarian? I'd take Talia's, but the guys will need it to find our hostess." She leveled a narrowed glance at Harm. "And you *will* find her."

Harm's jaw hardened. "Damn right, we will."

Jamba nodded. "You will have to take Mr. Wiggins into Nairobi. He'll stand a better chance there."

Marly sat on the ground with Mr. Wiggins's big head in her lap. "I hope he makes it. He's in pretty bad shape."

The men helped lift the leopard into the bed of Jamba's truck. Marly and Angela climbed in with Jamba, and he drove them out of the compound, headed for Nairobi.

Harm ran back into the lodge and up to his room, where he pulled on his boots, slipped his shoulder holster over his arms and secured the buckles. Then he checked his pistol, slipped it into his jacket and added a couple loaded magazines to his pockets. He didn't know what he would be up against, but he wanted to be ready.

Back outside, he joined the other members of his

team around the resort safari truck. T-Mac and Pitbull had brought along their gear bags, indicating
they were packing longer-range rifles. Good. Pistols
were only good for close range.

All six men climbed into the truck. Big Jake took
the wheel, which was fine with Harm. He wanted his
hands free in case he was forced to shoot someone.
And he'd shoot a lot of someones if it meant getting
Talia back. Alive.

The road to the village seemed longer than before.
About fifteen minutes into the ride, Harm spotted another truck ahead. The men getting out appeared to be
armed. "Slow down." Harm pulled out a pair of binoculars Talia kept on board for spotting wildlife and
focused on the men piling out of the truck. All were
armed with military-grade rifles, possibly AK-47s.
And they were aiming at the oncoming truck.

"Stop!" Harm yelled. "Take cover!"

Big Jake slammed on the brakes and slid the truck
sideways on the road. Even before the vehicle came
to a stop, the five men not driving leaped out on the
side of the truck, away from the men firing on them.

Bullets slammed into the side of the truck, but so
far, no one had been hit.

T-Mac and Pitbull pulled from their gear bags the
M4A1 rifles with the SOPMOD upgrades they'd had
built specifically for special operations. Each man
took up a position on either end of the truck and
aimed at the men firing at them.

"Give them a warning shot first," Big Jake said.

"Like hell. They tried to kill us," Harm argued.

"We're not supposed to be armed and operational in Kenya. We don't have clearance," Big Jake reminded them.

"They don't know that," Harm said, but he waited and let T-Mac and Pitbull work their sniper magic.

They aimed and fired almost simultaneously, kicking up the dust at the gunmen's feet.

Apparently, it didn't make a difference. They continued firing, peppering the truck with more bullet holes.

All six SEALs hunkered behind the relative safety of the big metal truck. They had distance on their side. Their rifles were modified to fire accurately at much longer distances than the AK-47s being used by their opponents.

"Okay, they got their warning. Make them believers," Big Jake said.

Harm wished he was the one with the sniper rifle. Waiting was hard. But he knew the two men on it were the best on the team.

Pitbull and T-Mac took aim and fired.

Two of the men who'd been showering them with bullets from their thirty-round banana clips suddenly stopped. One dropped to the ground, his weapon clattering to the dirt. He lay still. Probably dead.

The other screamed, flung his rifle to the side and fell, clutching at his leg.

Five other men turned and ran, scattering across a broad field.

"Should we take them down?" Pitbull asked.

"No. They're not stopping to set up defensive positions. My bet is they're not trained military men." Big Jake waited a few more minutes to make sure no one else was going to fire on them. Then he climbed into the truck and started the engine. "Let's go see what we caught."

The men climbed aboard, rifles and pistols trained on the truck ahead as they closed the distance between them.

The man on the ground who had been clutching at his leg crawled toward the rifle he'd thrown, wincing and moaning as he pulled himself through the dirt.

Harm leaped out of the truck and stepped on the weapon before the man could lift it and fire at them.

"Don't shoot!" he yelled and raised his hands high. "Don't shoot."

"We'll shoot if anyone else shoots at us," Harm said, pointing his pistol at the injured man.

"They're all gone." The man went back to clutching his leg. "I'm bleeding to death. They left me to die."

"Hey, guys, get a load of this." Diesel stood at the rear of the broken-down truck, lifting a tarp with the barrel of his pistol.

Harm remained where he was, with his foot on the rifle, while the others crowded around the truck and peered into the bed.

"Holy hell!" Big Jake exclaimed. "We should have shot every last one of those guys."

"Why?"

"They're the poachers." Big Jake lifted an object out of the truck and held it up.

Harm's gut twisted.

The long ivory tusk had to belong to the dead elephant they'd come across the day before.

"Where were you taking this?" Big Jake carried the tusk to the man on the ground.

"I don't know. They tell me nothing." He pressed his hand to the wound on his leg to stanch the bleeding.

"I'm not buying it," Harm said and aimed his pistol at the man's uninjured leg. "Where did they take Talia Ryan?"

The man stared up at him, a blank look on his face. "Mrs. Ryan?"

"Yes. Mrs. Ryan. Where did they take her?"

"I've heard nothing of this," the man on the ground said. "When did this happen?"

"Sometime in the middle of the night," Big Jake said. "Who else would take her if not the people she's trying to stop?"

"I swear, I know nothing."

"Then tell us who you sell the tusks to," Harm said. He wasn't convinced the man knew nothing about Talia's whereabouts. "Where were you taking the tusks?"

"I don't know," the man said, though he wouldn't meet Harm's gaze as he spoke.

"You're lying." Harm pointed the muzzle of his pistol at the man's good leg. "Try again."

The injured man on the ground pressed his lips together, refusing to utter another word.

Harm leaned close the man's ear and spoke softly, yet firmly. "I suggest you start talking, or I'll shoot the other leg."

"Don't shoot! Don't shoot!" The man ducked his head and scooted away from Harm.

Diesel, T-Mac, Buck and Pitbull stepped up behind him, blocking any escape route.

"You don't understand," the injured man cried. "They will kill me."

"Or we will," Harm reminded him. "Your choice. My finger is getting really tired of resting on the trigger. All it will take is for me to jerk that finger and I'll put a bullet in your other leg. At close range, it won't be as easily treated as the other gunshot wound."

"No, please, don't shoot." He cast a glance in the direction his comrades had gone. "We were to meet with our contact tonight."

"Where?"

"Outside the village, near the ruins of an old fort."

"Who is your contact?" Big Jake asked again.

"I don't know. None of us know. He wears a mask and pays us well."

"He will be there tonight?"

"Not if he hears we have nothing to trade." The

man shot a glance toward the truck. "He will not come if we have no tusks or horns to deliver."

Big Jake turned toward the team medic. "Buck, fix this man's leg. He has goods to deliver."

Buck flushed the man's wound with bottled water, dug out the bullet, sanitized the wound and glued it with liquid bandage.

Meanwhile, Diesel and Pitbull looked into the engine compartment of the truck and fiddled with the wiring. A few minutes later, they were able to start the engine.

Harm lifted his chin slightly toward T-Mac, the team electronics guru. T-Mac gave an answering chin lift and hurried to his gear bag. He returned moments later, circled the truck once and then helped Buck half carry the man into the driver's seat.

"He should be good enough to get the tusks to his buyer tonight," Buck pronounced. "He lost blood, but the bullet didn't hit any major arteries." Buck faced the man. "You need to see a doctor soon and get on antibiotics to reduce the chance of infection and possibly losing the leg."

"I will." The poacher frowned. "You are letting me go free?"

Big Jake nodded. "On the condition you deliver your goods to the buyer."

"How do you know I will deliver them?" the poacher asked.

"Because we will be watching you," Harm said.

"And we won't hesitate to kill you next time." Harm narrowed his eyes. "And we'll make it very painful."

"Unless you are with me, how will you know if I delivered?" The wounded man winced as he adjusted his position in the truck's seat.

"We have ways," Big Jake said. "So, make sure you take your goods to the buyer. Your life depends on it."

Diesel and Pitbull loaded the dead poacher into the back of the truck with the tusks. The wounded poacher shifted into gear and drove the truck toward the village.

Harm stood beside T-Mac as the poachers' truck left in a cloud of dust. "You tagged him?"

"Tracker in the truck, on the tusks and in the poacher's clothes. We should be able to find them." He held up the tracking device reader. "Ready to roll?"

"Don't worry," Big Jake said as he started the truck. "We'll find Talia."

Harm wasn't as certain. "We don't know that the poachers are the ones who took her."

The men climbed into the back, and Big Jake took off after the poachers' truck, heading for the village.

T-Mac called out from the seat behind Harm. "The poacher turned off the main road." He leaned over and showed Harm the display. They were coming up on the road the poacher had taken.

"As long as we can track him," Big Jake said, "we should be able to find him again."

The big SEAL passed the turnoff and continued toward the village.

Harm spun in his seat, looking over his shoulder at the dirt track the other truck had taken, his heart hammering. "Aren't we going to follow him?"

"No, he needs to meet up with his compadres and make good their handoff. They were supposed to meet with the buyer tonight."

"Aren't we taking a risk they'll make the handoff early?" Harm asked.

Big Jake smiled, a thin, dangerous smile. "If so, the tusks are marked. We'll find him. I didn't get the impression our little poacher dude knew anything about Talia's kidnapping. I think we need to talk to the witch doctor."

"Good." Harm sat back in his seat and stared at the road ahead. "I have a feeling the witch doctor is more involved than just spreading rumors."

"My thoughts, too."

As they pulled into the village, women and children moved out of the road to keep from being hit. Big Jake parked in the village center.

Before the men piled out, Jake said, "Harm and I will handle this. The rest of you stay put. We don't want to overwhelm the locals."

Big Jake headed for an elderly man seated on the ground in front of a mud-and-stick hut.

Harm spotted the old woman Talia had questioned the day before and headed straight for her. He squatted beside where she sat weaving a basket with her gnarled hands. "Where can I find Gakuru?" he demanded, his tone harsher than he intended. The more time that passed and they hadn't found Talia, the more worried he became.

The old woman didn't look up, nor did she speak.

Swallowing his frustration, Harm started over, lowering his voice to a softer, gentler tone. "Mrs. Talia is missing. I need to find her. Please…help me."

This time, she looked up, her eyes widening. "Mrs. Talia?"

He nodded. "She was taken in the night. I need help finding her before it's too late."

The old woman shook her head. "Gakuru warned her. He said she was bringing bad juju to our people. She should have left when her husband was killed."

Again, swallowing the burbling desperation he could barely contain, Harm spoke in an even tone. "We can't change the past. But I have to find her. Gakuru might know where I should look. Do you know where I can find him?"

The woman's fingers continued to weave the basket, threading the strands in and out as if by memory. When Harm thought he'd hit a wall, she finally spoke. "His home is the building south of the village, a ten-minute walk by foot. You will know it by the mask on the door."

Harm joined Big Jake at the truck and climbed in.

"The village leader didn't have much to say," Big Jake reported. "However, he said head south to find the witch doctor."

"The old woman Talia spoke to yesterday said the same. She said the witch doctor warned her to leave and that by being here, she was spreading bad juju."

Big Jake snorted. "Yeah. A bunch of horse hockey, if you ask me."

The ten-minute walk south took less than a minute in the truck, and soon they were pulling up to the hut with the mask on the door.

A short, dark man sat on the ground in front of a cauldron, alternating feeding sticks into the fire beneath and stirring the contents.

Again, Big Jake asked the others to wait in the truck while he and Harm climbed down.

Harm reached the man first. "Are you Gakuru?"

The man glanced up, his eyes rheumy and bloodshot. "Who wants to know?"

"I'm Harmon, a guest at the All Things Wild Resort." Trying to keep the desperation out of his voice, he went on. "Mrs. Ryan is missing. We thought you might have an idea of where we can look for her."

"Why would I know where she is?" He continued to stir the contents of the pot. "Perhaps she finally heeded my warning and left Kenya."

"Why should she leave Kenya?" Big Jake asked. "This has been her home for many years."

A sneer curled the witch doctor's lips on one side. "With her husband dead, she brings bad juju on the people of the village."

"She offers jobs and brings in tourists for those

people to sell their goods to. How is that bad juju?" Harm asked.

"A lone woman needs a man to bring balance to her life and those around her."

"Mrs. Ryan doesn't need anyone. She's strong, has a big heart and helps others." Harm couldn't hold back. "She certainly didn't deserve to be singled out by you as bringing bad luck to the people of the community." He stepped closer, all pretense and niceness gone. "What do you know about her disappearance?"

The witch doctor straightened to his full height, coming up short of Harm by at least eight inches. "I know nothing, other than the fact that she should have left long ago. This country is no place for a lone woman running a resort by herself."

"If you are lying to me—" Harm reached for the man, but Big Jake stepped between them, placing a hand on each man's arm.

"He's of no use to us." Big Jake let go of his grip on the witch doctor and tightened his hand on Harm's arm. "Come on, we have work to do."

"If you've done anything to hurt Talia, I'll be back. Without my guard dog." Harm glared at the witch doctor before turning to follow Big Jake.

As the two men climbed into the truck, T-Mac leaned over the backs of their seats and showed them the tracking monitor. "The poachers' truck stopped a couple miles out of the village."

"We need to get back to the resort and see if Talia

turned up there. If not, we'll plan the coming evening accordingly."

"You think the poachers have something to do with Talia's disappearance?" T-Mac asked.

"No, but I think we might find out who's behind all the troubles she's had at the resort and on her safaris." He nodded toward the side mirrors. "Our witch doctor is on the move."

Harm studied the small, gnarled man in the mirror as he mounted a motorcycle and sped away. "Shouldn't we follow him?"

Big Jake shook his head. "I tagged him with one of T-Mac's tracking devices. My bet is he knows something and we'll find out soon what that is."

Harm sat back in his seat, his fist clenched. Too many threads remained loose, and they still had no idea where Talia had been taken or who had kidnapped her.

TALIA OPENED HER eyes to dark gray light filtering beneath the door of the room where she lay on a dirt floor. Her vision blurred, and she fought to keep from losing the contents of her belly. When she moved her head, a shooting pain radiated from the back of her neck through her skull. She gasped and lay still until a wave of dizziness passed.

When she tried to move her hands and feet, she couldn't. They were bound together with what felt like duct tape. Keeping her head and neck as still as possible, she flexed her legs, and her feet bumped into something soft.

A moan rose from somewhere near her feet.

"Who's there?" Talia said into the darkness, her voice rough and gravelly.

Another moan sounded, and the soft form at her feet shifted.

"Who's with me?" Talia asked again, the words hard to form, the sound coming out more of a whisper.

"Mrs. Talia?" a shaky, feminine voice said.

Talia's heartbeat stirred a little faster. She fought off the gray fog of semiconsciousness, trying to hang on for the sake of the other woman in the room. "Eriku?"

"Yes," she answered as if it took a lot of effort to force the word out. "Where are we?"

"I don't know," Talia answered.

Voices sounded outside the door. Men. They were speaking in angry tones.

Talia tried to turn her head and wished she hadn't. The stabbing pain made her stomach roil and her head spin. She fought the encroachment of fog seeping in around her vision, but it was a losing battle.

The door opened, but she couldn't stop her eyes from closing. In an in-and-out state of consciousness, she recognized one of the voices but could do nothing to call out. She felt her body lifted by rough hands, and she was flung over a man's shoulder. They carried her from the room and out into the cool night air. With her hands bound, she was unable to steady herself, nor did she have the energy to try. Her head flopped and the pain sent her into a black abyss.

Her last thought was of Harm and the joy he'd brought back into her life. She wished he was there, and she wished she could tell him how he made her feel. Too bad he'd never know.

Chapter Fourteen

"I count eight tangos, two trucks and a motorcycle in the center of the camp," Harm reported. He'd taken point on their mission to infiltrate the poachers' transfer of the illegal goods.

The camp was nothing more than a few tents, sheltered beneath camouflage netting and several stacks of crates that had been unloaded from the trucks. One of the trucks there was the one they'd allowed to leave earlier that day.

The injured poacher limped around the camp, leaning on a long stick, his gaze darting left and right. The man had to be scared out of his mind. Harm hoped so. He hoped they'd scared him so much he'd get out of the poaching business and go legit.

"We have another vehicle approaching," Pitbull said from his position observing the dirt track leading into the camp.

A shiny black SUV bumped along the ruts and entered the camp. A man climbed out of the vehicle, surrounded by four big burly men with AK-47 rifles. The five men entered the tent along with four of the poachers, the injured man being one of them.

"The gang's all here," Big Jake whispered into their headsets. "Let's move."

Harm waited for the others to come online with him. They took out the few poachers who'd been set up as guards on the perimeter. Not a shot was fired, but the men were silenced, gagged and tied. If all went as planned, they wouldn't be poaching anything ever again. The SEALs would turn them over to the authorities, they'd be tried and sentenced.

One by one, Harm and his team took out the men around the camp, carefully keeping it quiet so that the men inside the tent would not be aware of what was going on outside.

One of the SUV bodyguards stood at the front of the tent, his weapon at the ready. Another stood at the rear.

"Ready?" Diesel said, in position near the rear. At the same time, he and Harm moved, taking out the guards.

No sooner had he dispatched the man guarding the door than another bodyguard stepped out of the tent. He almost stumbled on his teammate on the ground. Harm slipped up behind him and clamped his arm around the man's throat, choking off his vocal cords and air.

The man slid silently to the ground, unconscious.

Voices sounded from inside the tent. Harm recognized the witch doctor's muttering, though his words seemed slurred.

"Remember, we need some of them alive to answer questions," Harm said quietly into the radio. Then he motioned for the others of his team to move in. When they had the tent surrounded, Harm, Big Jake and Pitbull slipped through the door and behind the guards gathered inside.

Shots rang out.

Harm pressed a knife to the throat of one of the burly bodyguards and held the man in front of him as a human shield. The only light came from a battery-operated lantern hanging from the center pole. It rocked violently as the struggle within ensued.

By the time they had the occupants inside subdued, three were dead and the others were incapacitated.

Harm performed a head count of his teammates. Everyone was there. All the SEALs were alive and uninjured. He breathed a short sigh of relief and concentrated on what they had in front of them.

The poachers had been quick to throw down their weapons after three of their compatriots had been knocked out. And the witch doctor lay in the fetal position, covering his head with his hands, mumbling in a language Harm didn't understand.

The man in the mask knelt on the floor, his hands cinched behind his back in zip ties T-Mac had brought from his gear bag. The two remaining bodyguards were secured with handy duct tape.

Big Jake grabbed the mask and yanked it off the man's head.

"Don't kill me!" he begged. "I wasn't even supposed to be here. I was just filling in for someone else. He said it was an easy way to make a lot of money. All I had to do was pay for the goods and leave."

"Who sent you?" Harm demanded.

The man glanced around the inside of the tent, his eyes wide, his fear evident. "I can't say."

"Yes. You. Can." Harm pressed the tip of his Ka-Bar knife to the man's throat.

The man moaned, his entire body shaking. "He said I'd be killed if anyone found out."

"Well, you've been found out and you will be turned over to the authorities," Big Jake said. "Are you going to let the man who sent you get away while you go to jail?"

The man glanced around at the poachers still alive and glaring at him. "What about them?"

"Oh, they're going to jail, too," Big Jake bluffed.

Harm didn't have any idea what happened to poachers and middlemen in Kenya. But Big Jake was probably close enough to right for them to believe him.

"Did you stop to think that whoever sent you knew this would be a bad night?" Harm leaned close to the man. "He sent you to take the fall for him. Are you going to let him get away with it? He'll be a free man, while you languish in some hellhole of a prison."

"No." The man shook his head. "He wouldn't do that."

"But he did." Harm waved a hand around the room. "Look around you. You should be dead right now, if we didn't let you live. *He* would have been dead had he come."

The man hesitated, his gaze shooting back and forth as if he was searching for an escape. Finally, he stared at Harm and said, "Krause sent me."

"Jim Krause?" Harm frowned. "Mrs. Ryan's neighbor?"

The man nodded. "He wanted me to negotiate this deal while he took care of other business."

"What other business?" Harm asked, his tone low, strained. His heart hammered against his ribs. He knew the answer without the man actually saying it.

"He wanted to get Talia Ryan out of the way. She was messing up his operation by stirring up the local women."

Harm's heart squeezed hard inside his chest. "What operation?"

"He takes rich people on safari hunts for a lot of money and then turns the dead animals over to the poachers to scavenge what they want."

"The bastard," Harm bit out.

Big Jake picked up the thread and unraveled it further. "And then he masquerades as this silent middleman brokering the illegal goods from the poachers and sells them to the Chinese?"

The man nodded. He glanced at the poachers. "He makes it look like the poachers are the ones killing the animals, not the rich hunters."

Harm grabbed the man by the collar and half lifted him off the ground. "Where is Krause now?"

"I don't know. He said he was going to take care of the women and make sure no one could take over the resort when they were gone."

The witch doctor moaned and muttered, "The only way to rid a place of pestilence is to burn it. Cleanse the bad juju with flame."

At the old man's words, Harm's blood ran cold through his veins. "He's going to destroy the lodge." He ran for the door. "God, I hope Talia's not in it."

"Don't leave without us," Big Jake called out. He pointed to the SEALs. "More duct tape. Pronto!"

While the team remained behind to apply liberal amounts of tape to their captives, Harm ran for the truck, sprinting a mile to get to it. He raced back to the camp in time for the rest of his crew to jump on board. He would have driven on without them, but chances were he'd need them to help save Talia. Now wasn't the time to go rogue and do it alone.

Once he had all the men on board, he floored the accelerator and sent the truck down the rutted track toward the resort, thirty minutes away.

Talia might not have that much time.

WHEN TALIA WOKE AGAIN, her head ached with a different kind of pain and her vision blurred no matter how many times she blinked. When she lifted her head, the room spun and she could swear she smelled smoke.

She forced herself to stay awake and not slip back into the dark fog of drug-induced sleep. "Where am I?" she asked aloud, not expecting an answer.

"In your wine cellar," a female voice responded.

Talia glanced around, glad she'd had the foresight to have motion-sensor lights installed at the top of the stairs. At the moment, they shined down on her and her companion.

"Eriku," Talia said. "Are you all right?"

The woman nodded. "Yes, ma'am, for now. But I don't know what they have planned for us."

Talia sniffed the air. An acrid scent assailed her nostrils. Her heart leaped into her throat. "Do you smell smoke?"

The other woman lay on her side, her hands bound with duct tape behind her back. She sniffed the air and then nodded. "That's what it smells like. Did Jamba leave a pot burning on the stove?"

"He would never do that." By then her head had cleared and her heartbeat had kicked into high speed. "You don't think…whoever did this to us…holy hell." She struggled to free her hands. "We have to get out of here. Now!"

"I can't move my hands or feet."

"Me either, but maybe we can if we work together." Talia inched over to where Eriku lay on her side, her hands secured behind her back. "Let me see if I can tear away the tape on your wrists."

Eriku scooted until her back was to Talia.

Using her fingernails, Talia worked at the tape, searching for the end, praying she could find it and easily unwrap it to free Eriku. Why did it have to be so difficult? She scrambled furiously as the smoke thickened. Just when she was about to give up, she found the end and tore at the tape, clumsily unwinding it from around the young woman's wrists.

She had the tape down to the last wrap when the door to the cellar opened.

"Play dead," Talia whispered and went limp, closing her eyes and then opening them just a slit to see a man standing at the top of stairs, silhouetted against the light from the kitchen above. She couldn't make out his face, but she'd bet her last dollar it wasn't Harm.

A flashlight clicked on and the man descended, carrying a stick with a wad of cloth on the end. As he moved closer, the biting scent of gasoline filled the air.

When he reached the bottom, he stood next to Talia and nudged her with his foot. "You should have listened to the witch doctor and left when you could."

The voice belonged to Jim Krause.

He reached into his pocket, pulled out a cigarette lighter and lit the gasoline-saturated cloth wrapped around the stick. He started for a stack of empty cardboard boxes.

Talia couldn't keep quiet. Her life and Eriku's depended on her actions. "Don't do it, John."

He turned, his eyes narrowing. "Didn't give you enough of that drug, did I?" Her neighbor shrugged. "Oh, well. Can't be helped now." He tossed the torch into the stand of boxes. "You'll die of smoke inhalation before the fire takes care of the rest."

"You can't do this." Talia pushed to a sitting position. "At the least get Eriku out of here. She's just a child."

"Like you, she's interfering in my operation."

"What operation?" Her eyes widened as realization dawned on her. "You're behind the illegal hunting expeditions."

"You're partially right. My clients pay a lot of money to hunt big game. But my other clients are just as eager to pay me for the prizes. You realize I can get tens of thousands of dollars for each rhino horn and elephant tusk?" He shook his head. "And it all looks like poachers doing the dirty work." He smiled. Flames licked at the boxes behind him, giving him the appearance of the devil rising up from a burning hell.

Fear gripped Talia's heart. "Killing animals is bad enough. Killing humans is murder. You don't want to do that."

"Hell, I already have. That rhinoceros that ran over Michael was the front end of a pickup truck. He got too close to the truth. I couldn't let him blab it all over the country. He was a damned bleeding heart, always sticking up for the dumb animals."

Talia closed her eyes, the pain of her loss hitting her again. "You killed Michael."

"I did what I had to do. He was in the way, like you and Eriku are in the way. I thought Michael's death would have been enough for you to sell and leave Kenya. But you didn't. I paid the witch doctor to scare you away. You didn't leave. I finally had to take care of it myself."

"What did you do to Mr. Wiggins?"

"I gave him some tainted meat."

"Tainted?"

"With rat poison. The cat was protective of your compound. I couldn't let him get in the way. As it was, he made it easy for me to grab you."

Smoke was filling the room, making it more and more difficult to breathe, but rage burned brighter inside Talia. "Bastard!"

Krause snorted. "Maybe so, but I'm not letting some holier-than-thou women stand in the way of my profits." He started past her, heading for the stairs.

Talia lurched to her feet, swayed when she couldn't balance and launched herself into the man who'd killed her husband and was destroying the only home she'd known for all these years.

With wrists and ankles bound, she didn't have much control over her direction and speed, but she managed to clip the man in the backs of his knees.

Talia hit the floor on her shoulder. Her forehead bounced off the concrete and she nearly passed out.

But she didn't. And she witnessed Krause falling toward the stairs. He didn't have time to put out his hands to break his fall. His head hit the first step, and he lay still.

Eriku coughed. "We have to get out of here." She scooted over to where Talia lay on the ground. "You can't pass out now. Finish untying me so that I can free you, too."

Talia's head swam and her eyes and lungs stung, but she worked the rest of the tape free of Eriku's wrists.

When she pulled the last strand off Eriku's skin, the young woman gasped. But she didn't stop to cry at the pain; she tore at the tape on Talia's wrists.

"Don't," Talia said. "You don't have time. Get out before you're overcome by smoke."

"I'm not leaving you." Eriku coughed, pulled her shirt up over her mouth and nose and finally found the end of the tape. With quick efficiency, she unwound the tape from around Talia's wrists and ripped it free of her skin.

Talia bit down hard on her lip to keep from crying out. Losing a little skin was better than losing her life. As soon as her hands were free, she worked at the tape around her ankles while Eriku worked hers.

Talia freed herself sooner and helped Eriku work hers free. By then, the cellar was thick with smoke.

The only thing saving them was that they were lying on the floor.

Talia pulled her shirt up over her mouth and blinked. Tears streamed from her eyes, the smoke making it impossible to see and breathe. But if they didn't get out of the lodge in the next minute, they'd die. She crawled past Krause and motioned for Eriku to go first up the stairs.

Eriku scrambled upward, disappearing into the kitchen above.

Talia started after her and had gone up several steps when something snagged her ankle and pulled her back down the steps.

"No! You have to die," Krause said, his voice hoarse. He coughed and yanked harder at her ankle, dragging her back down into the smoke-filled cellar.

Talia screamed and kicked, but she couldn't free her ankle from the man's iron grip.

Chapter Fifteen

Harm's heart ached in his chest. He could see the flames reaching into the sky well before Big Jake pulled the truck into the resort compound. "Hurry!"

"I'm going as fast as I can," Big Jake said. As he brought the truck to a screeching halt in front of the burning lodge, a woman stumbled out of the main building and fell to the ground. Silhouetted against the flames, her face wasn't visible.

Harm leaped from his seat and ran toward her. When he reached her, he realized it wasn't Talia, but Eriku.

He rolled her onto her back and gripped her face between his palms. "Where's Talia?"

Eriku coughed and pointed toward the lodge. "In…the…wine cellar." She rolled to her side and coughed uncontrollably.

Harm yelled for Buck. "This woman needs help!" And he ran for the lodge.

Pitbull, Diesel, Big Jake and T-Mac raced up alongside him.

Big Jake grabbed his arm. "You can't go in there. It's an inferno."

"I have to. Talia's in the wine cellar. I have to get her out."

"Then come around the back. Take the shorter route to the kitchen and the cellar door." Big Jake led the way around the burning structure to the rear entrance, where the supplies were unloaded into the kitchen.

The back door was open. Flames rose up inside the kitchen, and the heat was staggering.

Harm stopped Big Jake at the door. "I'm going in. Don't follow." He didn't wait for his teammate's response but dived into hell, determined to come out with Talia or not at all.

On his way through the kitchen, he grabbed a dish towel, quickly soaked it in the sink and pressed it to his nose. Hunkering low to avoid the thickening smoke, he felt his way to where he remembered seeing the door that led down into the wine cellar.

It was open, and he could hear sounds coming up from below.

"Let go!" Talia yelled.

His pulse racing, Harm ran down the steps. The smoke was so thick. At first, he couldn't see Talia. Then through the haze, he noticed a jumble of arms and legs twisting about on the floor.

John Krause had her pinned to the ground. He pulled back his fist, ready to punch her in the face.

Rage ripped through Harm. He threw himself at the man, knocking him over before he could hit Talia.

"Talia, get out!" Harm yelled.

Krause swung at him.

Harm dodged the hit and landed a fist in the man's gut.

When Krause doubled over, Harm brought his knee up sharply and hit him in the face, breaking the man's nose. Krause crumpled to the ground, limp.

Smoke choked Harm, but he couldn't give up now. Talia wasn't moving.

He scooped her into his arms and ran up the steps and into what appeared to be a wall of flames. He didn't stop, racing through the fiery kitchen, his lungs burning, his eyes stinging. He couldn't remember which direction to run. The smoke made it impossible to see.

Hands reached out to guide him, pulling him through the maze of counters and islands and out the back door into the blessedly clean, smoke-free air.

Pitbull took Talia from Harm's arms and laid her on the ground, away from the flame-engulfed building.

Harm stumbled along beside him and collapsed in the dirt beside Talia. He coughed, trying to get the smoke out of his lungs. Then he leaned over her. "Sweetheart, tell me you're alive. Please."

She didn't respond.

He cupped her cheek and brushed his thumb across her lips. "Please don't die. I want to get to know you better. I want to take you out on a date. I'll quit the SEALs and stay with you in Africa, if that's what you want. I'll do anything, just don't die on me."

Harm watched her face in the light from the burning building.

Her eyelashes fluttered.

Harm's heart stopped beating and he held his breath. "Talia? Did you hear me?"

"Every word," she whispered, her voice hoarse, her eyes opening. Then she doubled up, coughing.

Buck arrived and squatted on the ground beside her. He handed her a bottle of water. "Drink a little of this."

Talia took the bottle and swallowed a sip. Then she coughed again, tears streaming from her eyes. "I thought I would die in that cellar," she said finally.

"You almost did." Harm smoothed her sooty hair from her forehead. "Welcome back." He pressed his lips to hers in a featherlight kiss and then sat up.

Pitbull knelt in the dirt beside them. "I put in a call to Marly on the satellite phone. They made it to Nairobi. She'll inform the authorities about the fire, and the wildlife management folks will collect the men we left tied up."

Talia frowned. "You left men tied up?"

"The poachers, the witch doctor and Krause's substitute middleman," Harm said. "We thought they might know where you were."

"And they did?" She glanced around at the SEAL team. "You found me."

"The witch doctor gave us the clue. He said the only way to cleanse the juju was to burn it." Harm pressed his lips into a tight line. "I figured Krause would torch the resort."

Talia glanced at the burning lodge. "He succeeded."

"A building can be rebuilt." Harm tucked a strand of her hair back behind her ear. "There's no replacing you."

She captured his hand in hers and pressed a kiss to his palm.

Pitbull leaned close. "You'll be glad to hear that Mr. Wiggins is going to be okay. Whatever poison was in him wasn't enough to kill him."

"Rat poison," Talia said and closed her eyes. "That bastard Krause poisoned the cat. He's behind all the poaching around here."

"We got a full confession out of Krause's stooge."

"He killed Michael." Talia pushed up to a sitting position. "Michael wasn't trampled by a rhino. He was run over by Krause's truck."

"Bastard," Big Jake said.

"I hope he rots in hell," Diesel agreed.

"He will," T-Mac said. "Right after you got Talia out of the lodge, the ceiling in the kitchen collapsed. We couldn't have saved Krause if we'd wanted to."

Harm rose to his feet. Talia raised her hand to him. He helped her to stand and slipped his arm around her waist to steady her. "I'm sorry we didn't get here in time to save the lodge."

She shook her head. "You got here in time to save me. That's all that matters." She leaned into him. "Thank you."

"We almost didn't make it." Harm's arm tightened. "It made me realize something."

"Oh, yeah?" She looked up at him in the light from the blaze. "What's that?"

"I know we've only known each other for a short time…" He drew in a deep breath and continued. "But what I know, I fell in love with." He smiled down at her. "I don't want it to end."

Talia wrapped her arms around him and held tight. "Me either. Staring death in the face made me want to live. And I wasn't living, holding on to the past."

Harm stared at the fire, imagining a future rising out of the ashes. A future with Talia.

"I never thought I could love someone as much as I loved Michael," Talia said softly. "Until I met you."

"And I never thought I'd fall so hard for someone that I'd give up my career to be with her. But I would." He turned to her and looked into her eyes. "I'd leave the navy and find work here in Africa, if it meant being with you."

She cupped his cheek and smiled into his eyes. "You'd do that for me?"

He nodded. "I want to be with you, to love you, raise a couple little girls with black hair and blue eyes that sparkle in the sunshine." He laughed. "Listen to me. The curmudgeon bachelor talking about love and children."

Big Jake snorted beside them. "Another one bites the dust." He glanced over at T-Mac. "That leaves the two of us. The hold-outs for retaining our bach-elorhood."

T-Mac sighed. "I could have gone for Talia, but she only had eyes for Harm." He patted his chest with both hands. "Talia, you don't know what you're missing by choosing Harm over me."

Harm swung a fist at T-Mac, clipping him lightly in the shoulder. "Face it, T-Mac, you never had a chance with her."

Talia laughed and coughed. "Your soul mate is out there. You just have to wait and recognize her when she comes along."

"Like Harm recognized his?" Big Jake asked. "I don't think he knew it at first. He should have. I could see the fear in his eyes. The fear of falling for someone. But he seems to be okay."

"It didn't hurt as bad as I thought it would," Harm admitted. "But then, I didn't lose her. If I had, it would have hurt a helluva lot more." He leaned down and kissed Talia.

"You are my soul mate. I never want to let you go."

"Sweetie, you don't have to. I'm yours, if you want me."

"Oh, hell yeah," he said.

"And you don't have to give up your career in the navy."

"No? But what about the resort?" Harm waved his hand at the burning lodge. "We can rebuild. I'm pretty handy with a hammer."

She shook her head. "I can donate the land and what's left of the buildings to the reserve. The animals need more space. The acreage that goes along with the resort might not be much, but it's something."

"Will you stay here in Africa?" Harm asked.

She shook her head. "I'd like to go to the States and back to school."

"There are some great colleges and universities in Virginia. Close to our home port," Harm suggested.

Talia smiled up at him. "I'd like that very much. Maybe I'll become a veterinarian."

"You're good with animals," Harm agreed.

"But before I go, I need to make sure Mr. Wiggins has a home at a refuge that will take care of him. He'd never make it out in the wild."

"Absolutely. I'd offer to let him come live with us, but I'm not sure about the laws governing wild animals in Virginia."

Talia shook her head. "He needs to stay in Africa where he belongs."

"Are you sure you don't belong here?"

"I can live anywhere my heart belongs." She touched her hand to his chest. "And my heart belongs with you."

Harm captured her hand and brought it up to his lips. "I love you, Talia, more than I ever thought possible. I promise to do my best to make you happy."

"And I love you, Harmon Payne. You proved to me that my heart is big enough to love again."

* * * * *

COMING NEXT MONTH FROM
⬡ HARLEQUIN®

INTRIGUE

Available September 18, 2018

#1809 ROGUE GUNSLINGER
Whitehorse, Montana: The Clementine Sisters • by B.J. Daniels
Bestselling author TJ Clementine is terrified when her "biggest fan" begins
sending her threatening letters. Only ruggedly handsome loner Silas Walker
can protect her...but can she trust him?

#1810 HIDEAWAY AT HAWK'S LANDING
Badge of Justice • by Rita Herron
Fearing for her child's life, Dr. Mila Manchester is forced to help a kidnapper,
which lands her in FBI custody. She will have to tell lawyer Brayden Hawk
her darkest secrets if she wants to recover her little girl.

#1811 KIDNAPPED AT CHRISTMAS
Crisis: Cattle Barge • by Barb Han
Meg Anderson walks back into bachelor Wyatt Jackson's life with a child
he never knew existed. Will Wyatt be able to protect Meg and his daughter
from a past Meg fought hard to forget?

#1812 RESCUED BY THE MARINE
by Julie Miller
Former Marine Jason Hunt is hired to recover Samantha Eddington,
a missing heiress. Jason failed to rescue a kidnapped woman during
his service. Will he be able to protect Sam...or is history destined to
repeat itself?

#1813 DANGER ON DAKOTA RIDGE
Eagle Mountain Murder Mystery • by Cindi Myers
DEA agent Rob Allerton is the only person who can help Paige Riddell, but
she wants nothing to do with him. Sparks fly between them, but the men
who are stalking Paige will do whatever it takes to keep her silent.

#1814 WYOMING COWBOY JUSTICE
Carsons & Delaneys • by Nicole Helm
The Carsons and the Delaneys have been at odds for as long as anyone
can remember. Yet when a Delaney is killed, Deputy Laurel Delaney turns to
Grady Carson for help. Will their teamwork be enough to find the killer and
keep an innocent man out of jail?

**YOU CAN FIND MORE INFORMATION ON UPCOMING HARLEQUIN® TITLES,
FREE EXCERPTS AND MORE AT WWW.HARLEQUIN.COM.**

HICNM0918

Get 4 FREE REWARDS!

We'll send you 2 FREE Books plus 2 FREE Mystery Gifts.

Harlequin® Intrigue books feature heroes and heroines that confront and survive danger while finding themselves irresistibly drawn to one another.

FREE
Value Over
$20

INTRIGUE

Author Tessa Jane Clementine, known by her readers as TJ St. Clair, is receiving threatening letters from a man claiming to be her biggest fan. Silas Walker, a handsome loner, is the only person who can protect her, but can she trust him?

Read on for a sneak preview of
Rogue Gunslinger
by New York Times *bestselling author B.J. Daniels.*

Chapter One

The old antique Royal typewriter clacked with each angry stroke of the keys. Shaking fingers pounded out livid words onto the old discolored paper. As the fury built, the fingers moved faster and faster until the keys all tangled together in a metal knot that lay suspended over the paper.

With a curse of frustration, the metal arms were tugged apart and the sound of the typewriter resumed in the small room. Angry words burst across the page, some letters darker than others as the keystrokes hit like a hammer. Other letters appeared lighter, some dropping down a half line as the fingers slipped from the worn keys. A bell sounded at the end of each line as the carriage was returned with a clang, until the paper was ripped from the typewriter.

Read in a cold, dark rage, the paper was folded hurriedly, the edges uneven, and stuffed into the envelope already addressed in the black typewritten letters:

Author TJ St. Clair
Whitehorse, Montana

The stamp slapped on, the envelope sealed, the fingers still shaking with expectation for when the novelist opened it. The fan rose and smiled. Wouldn't Ms. St. Clair, aka Tessa Jane Clementine, love this one.

***

TJ St. Clair hated conference calls. Especially this conference call.

"I know it's tough with your book coming out before Christmas," said Rachel the marketing coordinator, her voice sounding hollow on speakerphone in TJ's small New York City apartment.

"But I don't have to tell you how important it is to do as much promo as you can this week to get those sales where you want them," Sherry from Publicity and Events added.

TJ held her head and said nothing for a moment. "I'm going home for the holidays to be with my sisters, who I haven't seen in months." She started to say she knew how important promoting her book was, but in truth she often questioned if a lot of the events really made that much difference—let alone all the social media. If readers spent as much time as TJ had to on social media, she questioned how they could have time to read books.

"It's the threatening letters you've been getting, isn't it?" her agent Clara said.

She glanced toward the window, hating to admit that the letters had more than spooked her. "That is definitely part of it. They have been getting more…detailed and more threatening."

"I'm so sorry, TJ," Clara said and everyone added in words of sympathy.

"You've spoken to the police?" her editor, Dan French, asked.

"There is nothing they can do until…until the fan acts on the threats. That's another reason I want to go to Montana."

For a few beats there was silence. "All right. I can speak to Marketing," Dan said. "We'll do what we can from this end."

Don't miss
Rogue Gunslinger *by B.J. Daniels,*
available October 2018 wherever
Harlequin® Intrigue books and ebooks are sold.

Need an adrenaline rush from nail-biting tales
(and irresistible males)?

Check out **Harlequin Intrigue®**
and **Harlequin® Romantic Suspense** books!

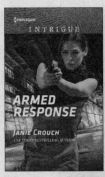

New books available every month!

CONNECT WITH US AT:

Facebook.com/groups/HarlequinConnection

f Facebook.com/HarlequinBooks

Twitter.com/HarlequinBooks

Instagram.com/HarlequinBooks

Pinterest.com/HarlequinBooks

ReaderService.com

**ROMANCE WHEN
YOU NEED IT**

SGENRE2018

Love Harlequin romance?

DISCOVER.

Be the first to find out about promotions, news and exclusive content!

Facebook.com/HarlequinBooks

Twitter.com/HarlequinBooks

Instagram.com/HarlequinBooks

Pinterest.com/HarlequinBooks

ReaderService.com

EXPLORE.

Sign up for the Harlequin e-newsletter and download a free book from any series at **TryHarlequin.com.**

CONNECT.

Join our Harlequin community to share your thoughts and connect with other romance readers!
Facebook.com/groups/HarlequinConnection

HARLEQUIN®

**ROMANCE WHEN
YOU NEED IT**

HSOCIAL2018

Earn points on your purchase of new Harlequin books from participating retailers.

Turn your points into **FREE BOOKS** of your choice!

Join for FREE today at
www.HarlequinMyRewards.com.

Harlequin My Rewards is a free program (no fees) without any commitments or obligations.

MYR18